The Virtual R
Series/Book

# The
# Deadly
# Maze

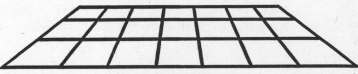

A Novel

## Bill Kritlow

Publishers Since 1798

**THOMAS NELSON PUBLISHERS**
Nashville • Atlanta • London • Vancouver

Published in Nashville, Tennessee, by Thomas Nelson, Inc., Publishers, and distributed in Canada by Word Communications, Ltd., Richmond, British Columbia, and in the United Kingdom by Word (UK), Ltd., Milton Keynes, England.

**Library of Congress Cataloging-in-Publication Data**

Kritlow, William.
    The deadly maze : a novel / Bill Kritlow.
      p.   cm. — (The virtual reality series ; bk .2)
    Summary: Kelly and Tim must rely on their computer skills and their faith in God when they try to rescue the President and his fourteen-year-old son, who are trapped in a virtual reality hostile to them.
    ISBN 0-7852-7924-5
    [1. Virtual reality—Fiction. 2. Christian life—Fiction. 3. Brothers and sisters—Fiction. 4. Computers—Fiction. 5. Science—fiction.] I. Title. II. Series: Kritlow, William. Virtual reality series ; bk. 2.
PZ7.K914De 1995
[Fic]—dc20                                    95-1705
                                          CIP
                                          AC

Printed in the United States of America
1 2 3 4 5 6 7 - 01 00 99 98 97 96 95

# CHAPTER 1

Gar had everything going for him. He had been told that for most of his fourteen years. He was athletically built, good looking with intense green eyes and nut brown hair, and he was the son of the president of the United States. His father had been in office for six years. But even though Gar had heard friends and the press talk about how good he had it for as long as he could remember, except when his mother died four years ago, he never thought they were right until now.

He stood in an incredible place—one alive with color—green plains, distant purple mountains, gold and orange and rusty crags. It was unlike anything he, or anyone else, had ever seen before. It was a place he had dreamed about—a place created just for him. Gar stood in Virtual Reality. He was in the middle of a vast plain—maybe old Montana or Wyoming—a place where the earth and sky unfolded forever in all directions. The old West—exactly what he had requested. Exactly. Now he did have everything he could possibly want.

He smelled the wind, the rich, sweet aroma of prairie flowers and grass as he turned completely around drinking in the new world. Gar knew it wasn't real. He knew he was still standing in the basement of the White House looking at images projected on the inside of his helmet visor; he knew the smells were generated inside the thick, black full-body suit he wore; he knew all this had been created especially for him by a man he had never met in person. But it didn't matter—all of it seemed very real and that was enough. It was peaceful, and he wanted peace. He wanted to be someplace where he could escape what was expected of him.

Nothing could be more peaceful than this. And Hammond Helbert, the programmer, had created it for him. What a friend he had turned out to be.

Suddenly Gar heard distant thunder and felt the ground trembling beneath him. It began as just a hint of sound, a pulsing growl from far off. But within seconds, the growl became a haunting rumble.

Gar spun around, his eyes scanning the horizon. At first he saw nothing. But then a thin, black line appeared on the eastern edge. It remained a thin line for only a heartbeat, then it bled over the hills like a tide—a living sea, waves pounding in his direction.

The thunder shook the earth—a pulsing quake rifled up Gar's legs directly to his heart. Hoofbeats. Millions of them. Pounding the ground. Churning up a cloud of dust that never once blurred the horde beneath it.

It was buffalo! Their thick heads and shoulders bobbed relentlessly, their hooves devouring the prairie like a hungry, black fire.

They were heading straight for him!

Hypnotized for an instant, Gar stood wondering what to do. He couldn't stay where he was. The herd would turn him into *virtual* hamburger.

He spun and looked for an escape route. The prairie stretched before him. Maybe this was a game Hammond Helbert was playing with him. Gar would be chased by the buffalo, and suddenly an escape would present itself—one leading to a great adventure. That had to be it.

Gar ran for it, keeping both eyes peeled for a way out.

But when he had been running for several minutes, he still saw nothing but more prairie made of more plains and hills.

The buffalo were gaining rapidly.

Was it a game? It had to be. His heart pounding as fast as the approaching hooves, Gar pushed himself as hard as he could. Even though he looked like an athlete, he wasn't one. He enjoyed sports now and then but preferred computer games. Now, with the churning hooves gaining on him, he wished he had put the Nintendo away and played a few more games of basketball. Glancing over his shoulder, he saw the sea of buffalo surge closer; the thunder raged louder. *So this is what grass feels like before the approaching lawn mower.*

He pressed the button on his palm—the trigger that took him

out of Virtual Reality. It was definitely time to get out. He waited for the images to fade and the visor on his helmet to rise, tossing him back into the real world.

Nothing happened.

He pushed the button harder. It was as if that real world out there did not exist and the only one that did was the one with a million buffalo bearing down on him. Panic-stricken, Gar pressed the left palm again. Nothing. Then the right one. More nothing.

Was the VR suit malfunctioning?

The herd pounded closer.

Virtual Reality or not, he was going to be hurt, maybe killed. After all, the reason the CIA, Special Forces, and NASA each got rid of the VR machine was because in each case one of their people had been seriously injured in VR. But only Gar and the programmer, Hammond Helbert, knew that—had his father known he never would have let Gar get the machine. "It'll teach me so much so quickly," Gar had told his father, who had been too busy to think long about his son's request. Now Gar wasn't so sure he had done the right thing. Maybe the machine had turned the programmer's good intentions in deadly directions. Hammond Helbert would never do this intentionally.

*Well, now,* thought Gar, his heart pounding in his throat, *if I'm going to die, I'm going to face it like a man—like my father would. Look it right in the eye. I owe myself that.*

His tongue pasted to the roof of his mouth, his legs about to give out altogether, he stopped, hesitated for a moment to catch what he could of his breath, then turned to face the stampede as bravely as he knew how. Gnawing on his lower lip, clenching his fists tightly, he waited as a million freight trains bore down upon him.

Not all of them would hit him. There would be only one at first—the one just ahead of him. The one with the bushy brown head and fiery, vengeful eyes, the one coming at him with the commitment of a locomotive, as if he were on a mission of destruction and Gar were the object of that mission.

Where was that programmer guy anyway? Suddenly another thought seared Gar's brain. Had he been set up? Had he been lured here just to be torn apart by buffalo? After all, he was the president's son. He normally had Secret Service crawling all over him. They left him alone here only because he was in the White House basement. Gar was vulnerable now—and if the Secret Service knew what was going on, they would be having several heart attacks.

Those fierce eyes kept barreling down on him.

What would it be like to be torn apart by a million hooves? Even *virtually* that had to be painful.

The herd covered the remaining distance in broad, relentless strides. Now he could feel their hot breath, the trembling earth. He braced himself for the world to collapse on top of him.

Then silence. The thunder like a rampaging river stopped.

Gar allowed his eyelids to part slightly, still afraid of what he might see. What he did see did nothing to decrease his fear. The buffalo were frozen inches from his face—a fierce image of heads bearing down on him, eyes blazing furnaces—stopped like a fearsome painting, poised to resume and crush the life out of him the instant life returned.

What had happened? What made everything freeze in time—except him? He could still move around. Run—now he could outrun them. His heart soared. Maybe he was safe! Was this his escape route? Maybe there was a new adventure just around the corner somewhere. But when he turned to run he only took two steps before he hit a transparent barrier—a glass wall. Without hesitating, Gar turned and ran to one side then the other. Each time he hit another transparent wall. Confused, he tried each direction again, and again he was stopped each time by a transparent wall. Was this a bug in the program, or was he a prisoner?

Did it matter? Either way the avalanche of buffalo might come to life any second and tear him apart.

◉

Bill Harkin, the president of the United States, was watching C-SPAN on the television in the Oval Office. The instant the vote in Congress was announced he and the two men with him exploded in cheers. "Great!" the president exclaimed. "Wonderful. That's a big one."

"The big one, Mr. President," one of the men agreed.

"You guys did a great job—wonderful job."

They both blushed under his praise.

At that moment, Terry Baker, the president's aide, poked his head into the Oval Office. He was young and efficient-looking and addressed the president with assurance. "Mr. President, your son's tutor is on one. She's agitated."

"That's all I need today. A great day in Congress, a mess in the classroom." President Harkin was a tall, imposing man in his early fifties. He had been an all-American fullback at the Air Force Academy at Colorado Springs, then a fighter pilot in Vietnam, then a senator and finally president—now in his second four-year term. His life had been a charmed one until his wife died two years into his first term—an accident while river rafting. She had left him with ten-year-old Gar—a child Bill Harkin did not understand. And, he was sure, no matter what the tutor wanted he wouldn't understand that either.

He was right. "He's where? Virtual what?"

The tutor, a motherly woman in her mid-forties, sounded tense as she told the president how excited Gar was about something. "He says he wants you to come in and see it. Says it'll only take a minute. Oh, Mr. President, he really asks you for so little. I think it would mean a lot to him."

"Come in? Come into what?"

◎

"Are you sure you want to do this?" Terry Baker stood beside the president as he eyed the black suit hanging beside other black suits just like it. Another suit was filled with his son. It seemed to be pacing nervously—like a caged cat.

The president eyed the message on the large, overhead screen. *Dad, come in for just a second. Please. I know you're busy, but it's important to me. You won't believe what I have to show you.*

The president was busy—always busy—and it was Terry Baker's job to make sure that he stayed on schedule.

"It'll only take a second," the president said, waving away his aide's concern.

But Terry wouldn't be put off. "You have got a full schedule today, sir. In fifteen minutes you have a meeting with your security advisers—there's at least three trouble spots around the world that could explode any minute. You can't miss this meeting."

"I won't miss it. It doesn't start until I get there." The president stared at the message again and frowned. "Gar, your timing's always right on target." But he took a deep breath and smiled. "It's been a great day for us. I'm going to take fifteen minutes to see what Gar wants, and then we'll get on with it. Fifteen minutes—no more."

President Harkin climbed into the VR suit, a tight fit for such a large man, pulled down the visor, and zipped it up. The instant all was in place the inside of the visor ignited with images. At first he wasn't sure what they were. He seemed to be inside a kaleidoscope until he felt the sensation of movement—rapid movement. He was in a tunnel, a slide, and he was careening down it feet first, colors and images whooshing past him. The slide turned, first gradually then radically, then again, this time in the other direction. The images began to spin around him— floor to ceiling, ceiling to floor.

The president was in reasonably good shape, but when the spinning began he quickly became disoriented and a little frightened. This was not just a simple carnival ride. He was getting sick.

Then it all stopped. A door opened at his feet, and he tumbled out the bottom.

He sat there for a moment to regain his senses, then slowly became aware that he was not alone. He heard a voice ask, "Can I help you?"

The world still spinning, the president began to focus on a boy's face pushed near his own. "Gar? Is that what you wanted to show me? You wanted to make me sick? What kind of son are you?"

"Dad?" Gar sounded genuinely surprised. "Is that you?"

"Sure, it's me," his father fired back. "Who else did you expect?"

"I didn't expect anyone, really. Are you here to get me out?"

The president eased himself to his feet and stumbled for an instant as the world continued to weave unsteadily around him. "You said you wanted to show me something. Then you spin me around like a top."

"I didn't ask you to come in here," Gar protested.

"If you didn't, who did?" Exasperated, the president shook

his head. "I'm getting too old for this kind of thing. Now let's get out of here, Gar."

"Do you know the way out?"

"What's that supposed to mean?"

Suddenly they heard another voice, a small, elfishly cheerful one whose singsongy notes seemed woven together by a satisfied triumph. "He means that he doesn't know the way out, and he hopes you do," it said. Hammond Helbert, the programmer, stood before them, an elf with large eyes, puffy face, pointy ears, colorful baggy clothes, and turned-up slippers—a crazy troll. "Of course, you and I know you don't know the way out, but it was good of you to respond to my invitation to VR."

The president was a man who knew only one approach to problems—attack. He took that approach now. "Your invitation? Who are you?" he roared.

Following his dad's lead, Gar also attacked. "Did you trick my dad into coming to VR? What are you doing to us? Let us out of here!"

Surprised, the president fired a question at his son. "You know this guy?"

"He's Hammond Helbert. The programmer. The machine didn't come with any documentation so he helped me."

"I did just that," Hammond Helbert chortled. "And your son was so eager to let me help."

"How did he get through security?" the president asked, his voice still filled with thunder. Only then did he notice the frozen wall of buffalo. "What are they?"

Hammond Helbert laughed softly. "One question at a time. Your son was kind enough to get me through security. I'm here electronically. After you authorized the machine for him, I contacted him by letter and showed him what to do inside Virtual Reality to allow me entry."

"I had to go through a thorny place with an invisible dragon," Gar related. "It was fun. Then I went to a round shed, a room with thousands of switches. After I flipped the right one I pushed a button. He appeared a few minutes later. I guess I was excited to finally have someone to work with."

"You opened the gate that allowed my transmission to come

in," Hammond Helbert explained. "I've watched this machine go from place to place, and each time I was able to find a willing friend to let me in. In the other places they were programmers who wanted to make names for themselves. But after being with them for a little while I decided that they couldn't give me what I wanted. When you, Garfield, the son of the most powerful man in the world, asked for the machine—well—has either of you ever had a dream come true?"

"Let me out of here, and I'll say yes," the president stormed.

"And when you, my dear Mr. President, agreed—well, you can imagine my excitement."

"I'm so pleased you're excited," the president said sarcastically. "I live to make you excited."

Hammond Helbert grinned. "Someday I'll vote, I'm sure."

"What about them?" The president indicated the wall of buffalo.

"If I let them go they'll crush you—virtually, of course. But three of the other services found out how painful such a thing could be. It could even be fatal to an older man. That's how I got them to give up the machine. It became unpredictable—just seemed to want to hurt people." Hammond Helbert laughed contemptuously.

The president declared, "My people can cut me out of this suit, you know. I'm in the basement of the White House. I'm not on some deserted island somewhere. They'll get me out of the suit, and then we'll come and find you."

Hammond Helbert laughed again. "I convinced the Special Forces people—the first people to have the machine, to build hundreds of storage batteries into the suit fabric, just in case the power went off—so that people could be extracted easily. Then, when they weren't looking, I wrote a little program that charges those storage cells and releases them into the person wearing the suit—quite painfully, I might add—if the fabric or the circuit is cut. The CIA trainee found out just how painful it could be. A mouse like you would be fried."

"Mouse? What?"

"Dad," Gar said, his voice sounding almost apologetic. "You didn't go through the digitizer, did you?"

"What digitizer?"

"You've come in the generic body."

The president looked at his hands, then his legs and feet. "I'm Mickey Mouse?!"

"A big Mickey too." Hammond Helbert laughed.

Gar explained, "It was a joke between Hammond Helbert and me. We kept changing the generic body—the one that you get when you don't go through the digitizer. The digitizer describes your body to the computer. Once we had Arnold Schwarzenegger—then Donald Duck. You are a big Mickey."

The president burst at his son, "Just helping him kidnap me wasn't enough! You had to make a joke of it."

Gar shrank before his father's outburst.

The president turned his attention back to the elf. "Okay, what do you want? Are you going to blackmail the world or something? Demand nuclear weapons—hand gun reform—"

Hammond Helbert smiled a wicked smile. "No—no blackmail. At least not for now."

"What then?" the president persisted. "Are you selling something? You wanted a private meeting with me?"

"No."

"Then what?" the president exploded.

The evil elf replied, "It's not you I want. You're just bait."

"Bait? Me? I'm the president of the United States. I'm not bait. I never have been nor will I ever be bait."

"Oh, you're bait, all right," said Hammond Helbert. "As a mouse you must know about traps and cheese. Right now you're more cheese than mouse."

"I'll rip this suit off myself," the president stated and immediately tried to tear the helmet off. But it was impossible. The helmet wouldn't go over his head nor would the zipper go down; they were both locked. The VR suit remained firmly in place.

The elf smiled triumphantly. In a tone that mocked both the president and his son, he said, "You'll like it here. And you'd better hope I succeed. If I don't, those buffalo will tear you to pieces. I understand you two haven't spent a lot of time together in the past. After that stampede gets through with you it'll be hard to tell you apart."

"You can't get away with this," the president warned. A wave of curiosity broke over him. "Who am I bait for?"

The elf laughed again. "Just a couple of kids and their meddlesome uncle. It seems strange to trade the president and his son—two people worth millions, maybe billions—for two kids and an eccentric genius. But no one beats me. No one—not twice. I want them, and now that I have you they'll be here soon."

"What happens to me and Gar then?"

"I don't know. Maybe I'll trade you for those millions. Or maybe I'll just crush all five of you."

## CHAPTER 2

U ncle Morty," Tim exclaimed, "is that what I think it is?"

Tim had just stepped into his Uncle Morty Craft's computer room. It was unusual to have such a room in a Wisconsin farmhouse, but Uncle Morty was an unusual guy. Having received his Ph.D. from MIT at age fourteen, Morty Craft had distinguished himself with a number of security-level government jobs focusing primarily on computers and electronic warfare until he had recently burned out. At age thirty-five he bought the farm next to his brother's and retired. But retirement was in name only. He kept busy—very busy. Not long ago he had been called upon to help the FBI and with Tim and Kelly— actually with them leading the way—he had kept deadly mutant bacteria at bay. Now he sat in front of his graphic workstation designing something for the approaching Fourth of July.

"What do you think it is?" Morty asked.

"A cow," the blond fourteen year old said, moving closer to make sure he wasn't missing anything.

"You do know your bovine."

"I've milked enough of 'em. But why is it red, white, and blue?"

"You know colors too." The cow was sectioned off; the white and red were in stripes with a blue square on the left, the upper part of the cow's rump. Since the graphic was a three-dimensional depiction, the colors adhered to the cow's contours, all with proper computer-generated shading. "Watch this." Uncle Morty aimed the mouse at four spots in the patch of blue. After a quick click, a white star appeared and remained in each spot.

"A cow flag?"

"Want more stars?"

"You're going to wave a cow?"

"Just paint one. Seems appropriate for around here."

"Paint Elvira?"

"Just one side. The one facing the reviewing stand. I'll wear my flag tie. We'll be quite the parade participants," Morty said smacking his lips.

"We were just going to decorate Dad's tractor. Maybe we could design it on your graphics system here. . . . No, Dad wouldn't go for it. He's not a fan of technology. I designed a new barn management system using computers to make the barn operation more efficient—I'll bet he doesn't go for that either."

"He's thinking about getting a tractor with a fax in it. He might go for barn management."

"A fax? What for?"

"Ask him."

"Well," said Tim, considering this new piece of information, "Dad, the hi-tech farmer. I'll have to think about that one for a while."

Kelly opened the door and stepped in. She was a year younger than Tim, and where Tim was long and lanky, Kelly was sweetly slender and athletic. She wore jeans and a sweatshirt on this Tuesday evening. Her auburn hair beneath a Minnesota Twins baseball cap streamed down her back. She saw the painted cow on the monitor screen. "What's that?" she exclaimed.

"Uncle Morty's Fourth of July entry," Tim explained.

"Can I paint her?" Kelly asked with sudden enthusiasm. "I've always thought cows were untapped advertising space. This could lead to *big* profits."

Tim laughed. "So this is hereditary."

"I'll have plenty of time," Kelly continued enthusiastically. "One of the kids at church is organizing an entry. I was just going to join him."

"Bobby Walker?" Tim asked. "He's been calling all morning."

"Bobby?" Kelly grimaced. "No—not Bobby Walker."

"That new kid—Bernie something?" Tim fired her way.

"Bernie Freeman."

"Mom won't be thrilled. She's already warned you about him."

"He goes to church."

"He's gotten in trouble at school and with the police, and he's only been here a couple months."

"But he's okay. Anyway, it's just an entry he's putting together. I thought it would be fun." In an effort to change the subject, Kelly told Tim, "Dad wants to see you. He was looking at your plan to computerize the milk barn."

"He was?" Tim gulped some air.

"Steady, big fella," Uncle Morty cautioned with just a hint of a jab. "Your chance at greatness has arrived."

"Dad looked concerned," Kelly chided.

"He might surprise you," Uncle Morty injected.

"He never has before," Tim said, showing a bit of his own concern.

Kelly's attention returned to Uncle Morty. "What are you going to do with the tail?" she asked.

Without answering, Uncle Morty dragged the mouse indicator down the cow's tail, and as it moved, red, white, and blue ringlets followed—all the way to the tip.

"Cool!" pronounced Kelly. "Let's do the same with her ears."

John Craft, Tim and Kelly's dad, sat in jeans and denim shirt in the "bill-paying" corner, an expansive, ancient rolltop desk that was his official place of business. All the things necessary to run the farm as a business were in the desk's drawers and cubbyholes. Twice a month John sat there making sure everything was still on track. Now he peered at a piece of paper with lines and boxes and explanatory words scrawled all over it. *Tim would rather do anything with those cows than milk 'em,* he thought.

Tim came through the front door. "You wanted me, Dad?"

John looked up and smiled. But long ago Tim had learned to recognize that smile as accompanying bad news. "Pull up a chair," John said.

Tim pulled up a straight-back chair. It was the most uncomfortable chair in the room, but he didn't notice. "What do you think?" he asked quickly.

"Actually, there are parts of it I like."

"There are?" That was unexpected. Tim grinned. "Then you'll do it? I thought you were going to tell me no." Perking up, he leaned back in the chair and winced when the hard wood dug into his back.

"No, we're not going to do it."

Tim's perk collapsed like a blown tire. "You're not? But you said—"

"Tim, we do three things on the farm. Milk, corn, and beans."

"I know—I live here too."

"Now don't be impertinent," John admonished. "We need the money from all three. But what's more, with the dairy we're dealing with God's creatures—cows. They aren't bright, but they are delicate—or at least getting them to give lots of milk can be a delicate thing. It doesn't take much to set them off. We introduce new things slowly—and when we do, we have to make sure they work."

Tim's eyes brightened. "It's too complicated," he stated, realizing his mistake. "I can fix that. We can go a little at a time."

"Tim, you're fourteen. I don't deny you've done remarkable things—you saved the world, I know." John Craft gave an impressed sigh. "But this is different. This is computer design and programming. You have to admit, you've only been playing around with computers since Morty got here, and that hasn't been very long. Granted you've got a lot of my brother's intelligence and creativity—"

"You're worried I'll kill the cows. I like the cows. I don't even mind the way they smell. I wouldn't kill the cows."

"Jesus gave me my family and this farm as responsibilities. Honoring him means I try my best to make the right decisions. I'll take this drawing to the college and have a prof I know give me his opinion. But even if he says it might work, we would probably need someone with more experience to make it work."

"But I know computers," Tim protested. "And you don't. Sure, this looks a little difficult. But it's really not."

John gave his son a conciliatory smile. "Actually, I've been talking to your Uncle Morty about computerizing the business side of the farm for the past few weeks. But this is different—"

"—and not as much fun."

"—and not as much fun. You're right. But we have to walk before we run."

"If I did that a while ago I would have never saved the world."

Tim liked the way that sounded. *Save the world.* It had a ring to it. And he was right. Had he and Kelly hesitated at all when they first encountered Matthew Helbert's Virtual Reality computer, the results might have been different. Hammond Helbert might have won, and if he had there would be far fewer people alive right now.

"Tim," his dad broke in. "I want you to come up with new ideas. A farm—any business—needs fresh ideas all the time. Right now, though, we'll go slowly. If it looks like it will fly I'll hire someone with experience to make it work. You can work with him or her. Experience is too important to ignore."

Tim's chest caved in. "Really? But that's not fair."

"It's not about being fair. It's about doing what's right for the farm and for you."

Tim was deflated. When he was younger, his dad had always entrusted him with responsibility. He would hand him a broom or a shovel and give him some brief, cryptic instructions and let him do the work. His father had trusted him to do the job right—or at least as right as a kid his age could. He had even let Tim do important things, like hooking up the milking machines or running the backhoe. It had only been recently—since Uncle Morty's arrival and Tim's awakening love for computers—that his dad had curbed that freedom. *He's jealous. And because he's jealous, he's going to keep me from working much with computers.*

But before Tim could take another run at his dad, the phone on the desk rang. John answered. "Oh, hi, Morty," he greeted cheerfully, but when he spoke again his voice sounded strained. "Again?" he exclaimed. "This is unbelievable. It's hard to tell kids who keep saving the world to milk cows and shovel manure."

Tim's ears perked, and he straightened attentively.

"Why do they want the kids?" he asked with deep reluctance. "But hasn't anyone else learned about that virtual stuff yet?" Then he sighed. Tim could see he was about to surrender; Tim was elated. "Well, Jesus took care of them the last time, I guess he'll do the same this time. Sure, I'll look after Elvira." He swallowed hard. "Did you really say the president?"

"Of the United States?" Tim exclaimed.

"Well, if it's a personal request—that's an honor, right? How am I going to tell their mother about this? It *is* a personal request from the president, isn't it? Well, then, we can't possibly turn down the president, even if I didn't vote for him—twice. Send Kelly back right away . . . oh, she has? A limo in an hour. Right." Then John Craft became even more serious. "You know, it's hard to get them to concentrate on real farm life when they're being whisked away in limos and jets. The only president *I've* ever met was of the local grange, and that hasn't hurt me one bit. When this ends they'll be left with nothing but lofty memories and barns to clean."

Uncle Morty must have said something, for it was a few moments before Tim's dad said good-bye and hung up.

John eyed his son. "Looks like the president wants you," he said, then smiled knowingly. "It's supposed to be an honor. I'm not so sure. It has to do with that Virtual Reality thing, so I have the feeling your guardian angel is going to be working overtime again." His expression became serious again. "This isn't easy for me, Tim. I want to keep you here—lock you in the barn or something. Maybe I should. Promise me that you'll be careful." Tim nodded. "Your mom and I love you—no matter who's asking to take you away." Then John shook his head. "Your mom's at a church meeting. She'll hang me out to dry if she comes home and you're gone. I'd better try to get hold of her."

Knowing she had less than an hour to pack, Kelly ran through Uncle Morty's fields, those he rented to her father, past a neighbor's outbuildings to a small cove on a lake. Since it was a little more protected and private, kids often used it as a swimming hole. She knew Bernie Freeman would be swimming there. While most of the other kids spent their summer vacations on 4-H projects and helping their families on the farms, Bernie did nothing but swim all day.

"Bernie," Kelly called to him as she ran over the last remaining hill.

A muscular fifteen year old stood on one of the diving platforms—a thick tree limb that hovered five or six feet above the water. The moment he heard Kelly's voice he called, "Be right there."

His dive was perfect. He hit the water with scarcely a splash and surfaced near the shoreline, just where Kelly stood.

"Hi," he greeted as he pushed thick black hair back from his smiling face.

"I wanted to come by and tell you that I might not be able to help with the parade entry you're putting together." She tried to sound strong, but there were two things weakening her— Bernie's nearness and the prospect of a plane flight in a little more than an hour.

"Parade? Oh, the Fourth of July thing. Right."

"You were talking about everyone getting together tomorrow night."

"Well, maybe not everyone," Bernie said, stepping from the water and standing next to her.

He was handsome, and his smile sent shock waves deep into her heart. "I thought you were going to get a whole bunch of the kids . . ."

"I have to be honest," Bernie said, his leaf brown eyes looking into hers. "I really only wanted to work with you."

"Me?" she squeaked. *Really, just me?*

"You and I seem to work together so well."

*Oh, we do, yes we certainly do. So very, very well.* "That way we could design what we want," Kelly said hesitantly.

Bernie stepped even closer and placed strong hands on her shoulders. "Now that's something to look forward to."

"Well," she whispered, staring up into those eyes. "It looks like I have to go—worse yet, I have to fly in a plane. I hate flying."

"You'll be gone for how long?" he asked, appearing heart-broken.

"I don't know."

"I'll miss you," said Bernie, and he drew even nearer. "I want to give you something to remember me by when you're up there in that plane—maybe it will give you courage."

The next thing Kelly knew, his lips were heading toward hers. Her heart began doing flip-flops in anticipation. But an instant later she surprised herself by turning slightly. His lips brushed her cheek. The fact that he wanted to kiss her was enough. When

Bernie pulled away, her knees nearly buckled. Fortunately Kelly caught herself before she collapsed.

"So you'll think of me when you're gone?" Bernie asked her, noticeably disappointed that he hadn't connected.

"Gone? Where? Oh, yes, gone. Plane—gone in plane—oh, yes." She brought her fingertips up to her lips. "Every minute," she said. She meant it too. She couldn't imagine the memory of those lips fading—ever. Even if the plane crashed. "I have to go now," she said haltingly. Then, suddenly needing to expend a reservoir of energy, she spun on her heels and ran.

She didn't stop until she threw herself onto her bed.

"Are you packing, dear?" her mother's voice called up the stairs.

"What? Oh, packing. Yes." Then she asked, "But I was wondering if you could do me a favor, Mom. Could you call the president and see if we could take the bus?"

# CHAPTER 3

Knuckles white as she clung to the chair's arms, chest tight as she dared not breathe, Kelly winced at every bump and imperfection in the Lear jet's ascent from the Eau Claire airport. She forced her head to peer out the window as the plane climbed steadily to fifty thousand feet.

"You okay?" Tim asked, sitting next to her.

"Perfect," Kelly said with a note of sarcasm. "After the last time I thought I wouldn't be so scared. I am."

Because Tim didn't reply and also because she wanted to forget about being in a small metal tube staying up just because a bunch of engineers she didn't even know said it should, she tried, and finally succeeded in, rekindling the memory of Bernie's kiss—well, his almost kiss. After a moment of intense concentration she imagined what the kiss would have been like. It now burned on her lips, her heart pounding again. But why had she turned away?

Maybe because she didn't want to have to keep the kiss from her mother . . .

Not only would her mother have found that kiss a little too mature—any kiss would have been—but it would have come from Bernie. Her parents didn't understand Bernie. He was above all this farm stuff. He had bigger thoughts—and he *must* be a Christian. He went to church and he talked about Jesus like he knew him.

But it would have been a wonderful kiss!

The plane bucked and bumped a couple of times as they broke through some turbulence, then settled. Kelly's heart bucked and bumped with it and finally lodged in her throat. Further reliving of the almost kiss would have to wait.

She tried to calm herself by focusing on their new mission—although she knew very little about it. Things had happened so quickly that she still wasn't sure what they would be doing. One thing was clear, though; it wasn't the FBI shuttling them around this time. It was the Secret Service—the presidential security detail. Strangely enough, they all *did* look like Clint Eastwood— much younger, but all four of the agents had that same stone-hard, committed expression. Kelly liked it. She even tried it herself. It was a welcome change from looking scared.

"You okay?" Tim asked again. "You look like something hurts."

"I was looking committed."

"You were looking like you *should* be committed."

She punched him.

The punch came just as the pilot announced that they had reached their cruising altitude. Agent Frank Holloway, an expressionless man of about thirty with Nordic blond hair and chiseled cheekbones came alive and stepped back from where he'd been sitting with the three other agents. "Let's gather around the table, and I'll brief you."

Uncle Morty looked up from a pad of paper he'd been sketching on. "Anybody have some colored pencils? I need red and blue."

"Got a red pen," Holloway said, digging into the inside pocket of his suit coat. As Uncle Morty took a seat around the small table at the center of the plane, Holloway handed him the pen. Morty took it and continued sketching.

"So, Agent Holloway," Kelly said, taking the seat next to Uncle Morty and trying to sound as adult as she could. "What do they have for us this time?"

"Not sure, exactly," Frank admitted. "As you know, President Harkin has a fourteen-year-old son, Gar."

"I read that Gar's a computer freak—a hacker," Tim pointed out. "*I'm* a computer freak."

Uncle Morty looked up from his sketching. "Has he got the Virtual Reality machine now?" he asked.

Frank gave a quick nod. "I've done some research on it. Army Special Forces got it first—after you guys were involved with it, anyway. They had a bad accident with it—hurt one of their top guys pretty badly. NASA had it next—again someone got hurt. Then the CIA took it for a while and the same thing happened.

The CIA guy is still in the hospital. The machine came up on a surplus list; Gar heard about it and asked his dad for it. He gave it to him."

"Did his dad know what the machine did to those people?" Tim asked and saw Uncle Morty nod, silently asking the same question.

"No," Frank said, "nobody thought to ask. We all looked at it as kind of a toy—we're still not sure if it's not just a toy. People got hurt, but people get hurt falling off chairs."

"So what's happened?" Uncle Morty asked.

"Gar is in there, and the president is with him," Frank said flatly. "He's asking for you to join them."

"Us?" Kelly questioned.

"We're not sure how he knows about you guys . . ."

"Why is the president in there? And what's the problem?" Tim asked.

Frank glanced at his watch. "He's been in there nearly four hours. We're not about to question what the president does. But we'd feel a lot more comfortable if he was out of there."

"Four hours. That sounds weird," Kelly said.

"We're starting to think it is."

Uncle Morty leaned back, his sketch forgotten now. "What happened?"

"Gar put on one of those black suits and entered Virtual Reality. A little while later he asked his father to come in there with him—he had something he wanted to show him. Since the president doesn't spend as much time with his son as he would like—particularly since his wife died—he went in. Now he is calling for you guys to join him before he comes out."

"Why didn't he come out and wait for us on the outside?" Morty asked.

"We've asked that question ourselves. The president's schedule is extremely crowded—he's a busy man—and he hates to stand around doing nothing for even a second or two."

"So this is not like him," Tim observed.

Frank nodded. "But when we try to communicate with him through the computer he just tells us that he and his son are involved in something revolutionary and wants you folks in there to help him with it. His son must have heard of you somehow. For whatever reason, the president has requested you—so here you are."

Kelly had a thought. "There are characters in Virtual Reality—Harve—"

"—and Barney—and Sonya," Tim added.

Kelly smirked. "Sonya especially." She remembered the black-haired, almond-eyed beauty who slithered away with Tim's heart during their last "virtual" trip.

"They could have told them about us," Uncle Morty finished the kids' thought. "I'm sure they have memories—and you have to admit, we're unforgettable."

"Well, we want you three to go in there, do whatever he wants, and get everyone out. This country can't exist without its president for long," Frank stated.

"What about the vice president?" Kelly asked.

"The vice president takes control only if the president dies or is physically unable to perform his duties—if he's in a coma or something. Not if he's standing in a black suit in the basement of the White House choosing to spend his time playing with his son."

"Just to get an idea of what we might find in there, are the NASA, CIA, and Special Forces training areas in Virtual Reality still active?" Morty asked.

"They were disabled," Frank said leaning back. "Gar might have found a way to get them working again. One of the men who was hurt was nearly electrocuted when his supervisors tried to cut him out of the suit."

"They must have cranked things up a bit since we were there," Morty said.

"We don't want the president getting stuck in there. He's in good shape, but he's nearly fifty-five—what *is* in there, anyway?"

Morty smiled. "Whatever the programmer decides."

"Who programs it?" Frank asked curiously.

"Anyone who gets his or her hands on it," Morty replied. "And it's not hard. Matthew Helbert did a great job of making it easy. The only way to find out what's in there is to go in and see."

"We tried to get a hold of Dr. Helbert."

"He'd make a good adviser—the best."

"We thought the same thing. We called but no answer. We sent local FBI but he wasn't home—or he didn't answer the door."

"Will you keep trying?"

"Sure." Frank hesitated as if a thought had struck. "Could Gar have programmed it himself?"

"If someone taught him. He might learn to do some of the basics on his own."

"Could he hurt someone knowing just the basics?"

"More likely someone could get hurt by stumbling into those NASA, CIA, and Special Forces training areas."

"So there *is* something to worry about," Frank declared.

"Maybe. We'll know after we explore."

Landing was as frightening for Kelly as taking off. Knuckles white, heart caught in her throat, from the moment they started to drop she didn't breathe until after they touched down at Fort Meade, Maryland. Her sigh of relief was delayed because they were immediately ushered into a presidential helicopter and then deposited on the White House lawn.

Seconds later, Frank and several other Secret Service men accompanied the Crafts past the White House guards into a large freight elevator to the basement. The elevator opened into a corridor. Unlike the areas above, the basement, though reasonably clean, needed a coat of paint. The walls were scuffed, the lights dim, the air musty.

They quickly brushed past two marine guards who stood rigidly on either side of the elevator door and a moment later entered an unimpressive but large room.

In the middle of it, looking like an orphan, was Matthew Helbert's machine—a small, eight-sided gray box with an expansive screen above it. In the corner stood the tall metal cylinder with "Digitizer" printed down the side. Although some things had been altered, the setup was much as Uncle Morty, Kelly, and Tim remembered it. NASA, CIA, and Special Forces may have used the machine, but they hadn't changed it much, at least from the outside. The only difference was the two figures in the black suits who stood on the wooden pedestal. Both seemed to be leaning against a wall. Three other suits hung on stands near three other pedestals. Morty, Tim, and Kelly were clearly expected.

Frank introduced them to Terry Baker, President Harkin's aide. His eyes were anxious. "Good. You're here," he said. "This is definitely getting serious. He's been in there five hours now, and this country isn't used to going without its president for five hours. Are you sure you're up to it?" he asked, doubt evident in his tone. Without waiting for an answer he snapped, "I want you guys suited up and in there quick."

"Have you tried contacting Matthew Helbert recently?" Morty asked. "He could be a lot of help even over the phone."

Terry turned to Frank, who immediately crossed to a phone that sat on a corner desk.

"Now," Terry said to Morty and the kids, "Is there anything else stopping you from going in there?"

Morty glanced at Tim and Kelly in turn, then answered, "Nothing."

"Good," Baker said with finality.

Frank returned from the phone. "No answer. I've ordered the locals to keep looking for him."

"Okay—well," Uncle Morty said to the kids, "Guess the time's come to see what we can do."

Tim and Kelly considered each other. Together they considered their last trek though VR—a world of snakes and dagger-sharp thorns where they were chased by dragons and knights on devil black horses. What would be waiting for them this time?

Uncle Morty turned to Frank. "Before we go through the digitizer we need to talk together alone for a moment—is there a room nearby?"

Frank wasn't excited about taking the extra time, and Terry Baker found the idea irritating, but neither could do anything about it. Morty insisted.

Alone in a small conference room the three stood beside a meeting table, Tim and Kelly waiting for Uncle Morty to speak first. "There's something going on in there," he said.

"What?" Kelly asked.

"Like he would know," Tim tossed back at her.

"Uncle Morty knows all," Kelly stated confidently.

"Not this time," Uncle Morty said, puzzled. "But I have a hunch that all is not as it seems."

"Like how?" Tim asked.

"Just a hunch—but be doubly careful if you find anything out of the ordinary. Of course, everything is out of the ordinary in there."

Tim and Kelly glanced at each other again.

"Okay, first we pray. Then we keep our eyes open and stay together."

They did pray. Although it was short, it said all that needed saying. They asked the Lord to walk with them, protect them, and to be glorified in what they did.

After the amen, all three returned to the VR machine room. While the others watched and waited, Uncle Morty, Tim, and Kelly each went through the digitizer then climbed into the black suits. They each donned a suit and helmet, pulled down a visor, and zipped everything up.

A moment later the darkness within the helmets exploded to light. Virtual Reality became their reality once more.

# CHAPTER 4

Dazzling colors danced and revolved around them, kaleidoscopic images folded, unfolded, and refolded—red, black, blue, green, yellow rolling over, above, and under them as they slid down a narrow pipe.

Kelly screamed, Tim whooped, and Uncle Morty did his best to keep from getting sick as he led the way. But it was getting increasingly difficult. Not only did the slide steepen, hurling them even faster, but as it did the colors spun around them more frantically—hypnotically so.

Suddenly the world opened up, and Morty slid feet first onto a western prairie. It was no ordinary prairie. Although there was the usual dusty grass on the ground, a wall of buffalo heads was frozen in the act of bearing down on a big mouse and a young boy. Morty recognized both of them immediately. The mouse was Mickey, the boy was the president's son.

"Gar Harkin?" Morty greeted with a kind of groan—the VR suit had done a good job simulating a hard landing on his backside.

The boy rushed at him excitedly. "You here to get us out?"

"I'm President Harkin," said the mouse, extending a three-fingered, white gloved hand. "*Are* you here to get us out?"

"Morty Craft," Morty introduced himself, shaking the president's hand. "Someone must have fixed that," he said under his breath.

"What?" the mouse asked.

"Used to be that visitors to VR couldn't touch—but that doesn't matter now. To get out of here all you do is press the button on the palm of your hand. Didn't anyone tell you? And why the mouse costume?"

"The palm buttons are broken," Gar said forlornly. "They don't work."

"Broken?" Morty exclaimed in disbelief and immediately pressed his. Gar was right. Nothing happened.

Suddenly he heard another voice—small and mocking. "Not broken—deactivated," it said.

Morty spun to see an elfish character, its pointed ears stiff, its smile a leer.

"I've dreamed of this moment—my revenge," it said.

"Revenge? About what? Who are you?" Morty was bewildered.

"You and those kids." The elf's expression changed to surprised anger. "Where are the kids?"

"They're . . ." Morty began but stopped. Where were Tim and Kelly? They'd been right behind him. Where did they go? "I don't know," he said mystified.

"You have to be together," the elf insisted, his voice sounding a bit crazy. "I planned it that way. You're not going to beat me again. Never again." A bony finger went up and pointed at Uncle Morty. "You can't leave. There's a boundary all around." Now he looked befuddled but still purple with rage. "I'll get them—either I'll get them or VR will." He turned back to his prisoners. "And then I'll take care of you!"

"Where are we?" Kelly groaned. She had been sliding just behind Uncle Morty, her feet only inches from his head. Then without any warning, Uncle Morty's tunnel turned left and Kelly's and Tim's went right. But they hadn't come to a fork in the tunnel—it was more like the tunnel had abruptly come to life, breaking off just behind Uncle Morty and taking Tim and Kelly somewhere else. And that somewhere else couldn't have been more different from the dazzling colors in the tunnel.

This place seemed draped in dreariness, cocooned in darkness—but not total darkness, more like persistent shadows. They were deep in a forest—but it wasn't a forest . . .

"We're in a swamp," Tim said, his voice barely above a whisper as if the swamp might hear him and become even more hostile.

It certainly was a swamp, and they seemed to be standing on the one bit of grassy land in it. Dark water lay all around them, and above them was a tightly woven canopy of limbs and leaves from which hung ghostly curtains of moss. Thick, twisted tree trunks grew up from the water to the canopy seemingly without the need for land. Creepy sounds surrounded them—croaking frogs, crickets, now and then the drum of flapping wings, and an owl's forlorn "hooo."

"There are snakes in swamps," Kelly groaned. "I hate snakes—lizards, too—all those things. I hate flying, and I hate snakes. I need to get a handle on my fears—but not today."

"We're wearing army fatigue uniforms," Tim said.

After a quick glance down to see that what Tim said was true, Kelly looked all around her—nothing was better in any direction. "I wonder where Uncle Morty went—we could use him right now."

"Things happened so fast."

"I guess all we know is he's not here," Kelly said. "We're on our own—again. But couldn't we be on our own in a mall or something? Why does it have to be a swamp?"

"How could we have gotten separated like that?" Tim asked, his eyes darting around nervously.

"It just happened. I guess there's nothing to do but deal with all this somehow. But why? Uncle Morty's having a great time with the president, probably being a big shot because he knows so much—and we're stuck slogging around in a swamp—with snakes."

Tim peered into the haunting shadows and listened. He heard the incessant rasp of crickets and a deceptively gentle lapping of water, probably as it caressed the many islands dotting the swamp. "It's like the Pirates of the Caribbean at Disney World."

"That's all we need—pirates *and* snakes." Kelly swallowed hard.

"Let's just get out of VR altogether. We'll try to get a hold of Uncle Morty from the outside. This place is starting to give me the willies."

Relieved to be taking the easy way out, Kelly was laughing as she pushed her palm button. Tim pushed his as well. "Try it again," Kelly said when nothing happened.

They did and again VR did not dissolve to black, the helmet and zipper did not unlock, and the visor did not lift—they remained in the swamp.

"I'm not sure I like this," Kelly said, her eyes darting from tree to water to tree.

"Is there any other way out?" Tim asked, his voice heavy with concern.

"I don't know of any."

"We're trapped in here?"

Kelly only nodded.

"Then we're not the only ones," Tim said, eyes locked on Kelly's.

"The president is trapped, too," she said, "*and* his son *and* Uncle Morty," Kelly hesitated as if digesting what she had just said. "Uncle Morty was right again—things weren't as they seemed. But to trap the president of the United States, then call us in here . . . what could that be about? And why are we here? Why aren't we with Uncle Morty?"

"What's that?" Tim pointed.

Looking in the same direction, Kelly saw it too. Something metallic reflected the light shimmering off the water. "A knife? Stuck in a tree?"

Both moved carefully through the thick, sloshy undergrowth to a broad, gnarled tree trunk, its roots reaching out from beneath it like pythons.

Tim exclaimed, "It *is* a knife!"

"It's pinning a sheet of paper to the tree," Kelly added.

The hunting knife was stuck at Tim's eye level, its sharp blade glistening in the dim light. It pinned an ancient document there. Grabbing the elk horn handle, Tim pulled the knife out, handed the page to Kelly, and stuck the knife in his belt.

Adjusting the page so it caught as much of the available light as possible, Kelly studied the document. Across the top was scrawled, "Welcome to Swamp School—Army Special Forces." Below was drawn a crude map.

"We're in the Special Forces training area," Kelly gasped.

"Ugh! We'll be eating snail burgers soon."

"Or snake-dogs. We have to get out of here," Kelly said. "I guess we follow the map."

Tim looked over her shoulder.

The map didn't have much information on it. The swamp area was defined by an irregular circle. At the bottom of it was a small *x* and a short line heading up from it. "We must be at the *x*," Tim said. At the end of the short line was another *x*, which was labeled "trapper's cabin—first checkpoint." "We probably get more information at the cabin."

"Look up here," Kelly pointed to another area of the map within the circle. A note scrawled there said, "Lots of alligators sighted here." "Yuck! I hate alligators most of all."

"And me without ketchup," Tim said. "Look here." He pointed to another note on the map. It read, "Watch for natives—bad news." Tim sighed. "Maybe eating snail burgers will be the high point."

"What's this over here?" Kelly pointed to another *x*. It was in the lower right, outside the swamp's outline. She strained her eyes to make out the label. "Control room," she read. "Control what? That doesn't make sense."

"It might to some Special Forces guy."

"That's weird," Kelly said.

"What?"

"The *x* is flashing sort of—look."

Tim squinted so he could see the control room *x* in the available light. It *was* flashing, but only slightly. Just enough to call their attention to it.

"What's it trying to tell us?" Kelly asked.

"Maybe it's the VR control room," Tim replied, a germ of a thought beginning.

"Where the switch is that turns the palm buttons back on," Kelly said softly, as if saying it more loudly would make it untrue.

"If we get there we could set everyone free," Tim whispered, the realization coming into focus—and with it, their new mission. "We use this map to get out of the swamp and then to get to that control room."

They looked off in the cabin's direction. The distant trees seemed less defined, the horizon, which had been the only source of light, was growing dim. "It's getting darker," Tim announced.

Kelly shuddered. "A swamp at night—not good."

"Well, let's go. The sooner we get there the sooner we get out of here."

Both knew that getting to the trapper cabin was more easily said than done—neither relished the swamp even in broad daylight, let alone when shadows were growing blacker. But there was no alternative. Grabbing their nerves with both hands, they each took a deep breath and began walking.

The wet ground sloshed as they walked through the ankle-deep grass, but the ground itself seemed solid. It was also hidden in shadows. There was no telling what lurked among the tree roots and tangled brush. But they kept walking.

As it turned out, the sounds were their worst enemy, at least at first. With the rasp of crickets as a backdrop, now and then an owl sent its haunting cry their way. The first time Kelly gasped, yet the second time she hardly noticed it. There were also the occasional splashes. The first splash somewhere out in the shadows caused Tim to stop and listen. "Maybe there *are* pirates," he whispered. But they finally decided it was just a fish leaping or something dropping from a tree—an acorn or maybe the whole squirrel. When they had gone about a hundred yards, the frightening things—the owls, the splashing, the random call of a crow—blended with the shadows and became just more annoyance.

The real annoyance was the light—there wasn't enough of it. The shadows began to blend with the trees and the brush, making everything a dismal gray. But the kids didn't slow down—they continued to plow ahead.

"So far so good," Tim commented.

It was obviously the wrong thing to say. The next step found Tim waist deep in water.

"Grab my hand," Kelly cried, reaching out.

Tim fumbled around in the mire for a moment but finally clasped Kelly's hand.

It took some doing on Kelly's part, but before long Tim had struggled up the embankment and stood beside her.

"You okay?" Kelly asked.

"It could have been deeper."

Kelly peered off into the darkness. "What now? No more path."

Tim nodded and did his best to work out a bruise on his knee.

The VR suit simulated his sudden drop too well. "I forgot how real this was," Tim groaned.

"Look!" Kelly suddenly exclaimed, pointing straight ahead.

Tim saw immediately what she was pointing at—a light drilled through the growing darkness—a flicking lantern maybe a hundred yards off. "The trapper's cabin," Tim said.

"How do we get there?" Kelly asked.

Surprisingly, the moon appeared through a break in the clouds. It lit the area but gave them no good news. They could now see that the path they'd been following had ended and the only way forward was through dark, murky water.

"I think we've entered the wading training area," Kelly finally said and cringed. "Can you imagine all the stuff slithering around in there?"

Tim frowned. "At least the programmers haven't made things slimy. I don't think I could do it if the bottom felt as slimy as a real swamp. Like the bottom of the lake back home."

Kelly groaned again. "Well, you're the guy—you lead the way."

"Spoken like a true feminist."

Tim prepared himself, said a silent prayer, and stepped into the water. Again he stood up to his waist in water, but this time, instead of trying to struggle back toward land, he took a determined step toward the light.

# CHAPTER 5

With Tim already up to his waist in the black water, Kelly held her breath and followed. Since she was at least six inches shorter than Tim, the water came to her chest. The way the VR suit simulated water brought a strange sensation. It wasn't wet, but it was cold and the currents buffeted her, at times forcing her to struggle to keep her balance. Walking through it was difficult; both legs and arms were needed to struggle forward. "If it gets deeper we're in real trouble," she warned.

"Do you think our air will cut off if we drop below the surface?" Tim asked.

"I hope we don't find out."

"Can you imagine this without the moonlight?"

Kelly didn't reply, but looked around. The moonlight *was* important. It glistened off the water and highlighted the trees and limbs and the twisting, meandering roots. Without it there would have been little more than black.

Even with the water's resistance, the swamp bottom's slippery irregularities, and the treacherous currents they made good time. After a while even the level lessened and dropped to Kelly's waist. Both she and Tim were beginning to relax when something reflected the moonlight as it slithered between them. Kelly was looking the other way and caught only a terrifying glimpse of it in the corner of her eye. As if to give her another look, another slithered by right after the first. A snake—a long, black, evil-eyed snake, its body buoyed by the murky water, its triangular head raised slightly, its tongue flicking at the air, testing—eased past her only a few feet away.

Kelly froze. "Snakes!" she cried.

Tim spun and stumbled. His arms flailing, the water splashing around him, he fought for balance. Unable to find it, he fell back first, his face disappearing beneath the waves. His arms still battling, his head returned to the surface.

While Kelly watched her brother struggle to his feet, she also watched the two snakes, now at least ten yards off. They stopped, circled for a moment as if assessing the disturbance Tim was making, then turned and headed straight for him. "Tim, they're coming for you!" she shouted.

"Oops!" he cried, spinning again and thrashing away through the water.

When the snakes had slithered by Kelly the first time, they moved with a broad, almost majestic, serpentine motion; now they shot forward like arrows—their heads and flicking tongues reaching out with grave determination. Within seconds they were closing in on Tim.

"Tim," Kelly shouted, "go underwater—quick."

Tim dropped, his body disappearing beneath the murky surface. Just in time. The two snakes converged where his head had been. But Tim wasn't safe yet. The snakes remained there, circling, waiting for him to resurface. The moment he did they would attack. Tim stayed down, but Kelly knew he couldn't hold his breath much longer. She had to do something.

She looked around for a floating stick that she could use as a club, but there was nothing. "Snakes! I hate 'em—everybody hates 'em! Snakes! Yuck! Lord, what now?"

But she had to do something—and quickly. Any second Tim would be coming to the surface. After a quick prayer, Kelly started flailing at the water—slapping it again and again.

The snakes swung around in confusion. They made their choice quickly. Eyes trained on her, tongues flicking at the air, they slithered in her direction.

What now?

They started out only ten feet away, so it would take them hardly a heartbeat to cross the distance. Kelly knew she couldn't run from them. Her only hope was to drop below the surface as Tim had done.

Just before she had to take that plunge Tim rose up gasping for air. "Slap the water—slap it hard!" Kelly cried.

He responded just in time.

Kelly's heart was about to explode, and the snakes were

within two feet when Tim finally started slapping the surface frantically. The snakes hardly hesitated at all but quickly swung around and headed back toward Tim, who was stepping backward to lengthen the distance the snakes would have to travel. When they had covered about two-thirds of the distance, Kelly battered the surface and the snakes turned again. When they'd covered most of the distance, Tim worked the water near him and the snakes turned back.

"How long can we keep this up?" Kelly called. "And how do we get out of it?"

Tim didn't answer. There was no answer to give—now none was appropriate. He saw something else that caused his eyes to widen and his jaw to drop. As the snakes pulled around toward Kelly, Tim pointed behind her.

Risking the approaching snakes, Kelly spun around.

Her heart leaped to her throat, her breath caught in her chest, and if there was a scream in her somewhere, it couldn't get out. Heading straight for her was the biggest snake she had ever seen. Like a living sewer pipe, maybe twenty feet long, the sleek body glistened in the moonlight. Its head, like the point of a giant's spear, was aimed right at her, pushing the water before it— heavy, determined—its eyes green as the moss and its stare hypnotic. It was no more than ten yards away.

"There's no time!" Kelly cried. No time to run from it. No time to outsmart it. It was closing on her fast. "Oh, Lord, what now?" she whispered, her lips trembling in terror.

She heard Tim slapping the surface. The smaller snakes must have been getting too close. But they seemed like a minor problem now, with the big serpent coming so quickly.

The closer it came the bigger it became—the more terrifying its eyes, the more diabolical.

Kelly shouted, "Oh, God, you have to do something!"

"Kelly, drop!" Tim shouted.

Instead, Kelly spun and saw the two smaller serpents closing in on Tim. But she did nothing; it was as if she was going into overload. She turned back to the big snake. Now it was less than five feet away.

"What are we going to do?" Kelly cried to her brother.

"Just drop. That snake will eat you whole."

Kelly could do nothing else. She dove beneath the surface just as the thick, menacing body slithered above her. She huddled in the black, cold, airless swamp water wondering what Tim was going to do, wondering how, or even if, she could help him.

Tim knew he was in trouble. The two smaller snakes were slithering toward him while the larger snake moved toward him now even faster. He spun around looking for something he could use as a weapon. There was nothing. He was still a long way from the next clump of land, and there was nothing but the three snakes floating on the water's surface. Any second now all three would be upon him. Tim remembered the snakebite he'd gotten the last time he was in VR. It hurt! These would hurt, too—maybe more. These would not only bite him, but the big one would probably wrap itself around him and crush him.

Not something to look forward to.

The knife from the tree! He grabbed for the handle and found it protruding from his belt. Holding it up, he saw its brightly honed edge reflect the moonlight with a threatening flash.

The two snakes were not impressed. They kept coming. Tim's heart tightened. He waited for just the right moment then swept the knife in a quick arc. He dispatched one of the snakes—took its head off. Then he took aim at the second one. He caught the snake near the middle of its body. A tactical error. Before it died its fangs fastened on Tim's hand. Though he quickly shook it off, the bite hurt—the suit's electronics ignited on the edge of his hand and pain rifled up his arm. He cried out in pain. "Tim! You okay?" Kelly was above the surface again watching her brother. The big snake was only a few feet away from him now.

Suddenly Tim realized he must have dropped his knife when the snake bit him.

His only hope was to find it. He dove beneath the surface, feeling for the knife. In the murky light he could barely see. But finally he saw light gleaming off something several yards away—the blade!

Tim dove, but before he reached it, the thick serpent's head imposed itself underwater between him and the knife, its body trailing behind. The head turned toward him and seemed to smile—a hard, executioner's smile.

Heart frozen, Tim backed away. The snake followed, its eyes riveted on his.

Tim didn't dare take his eyes away, but he needed air and would have to surface soon. He knew the moment he did, the big snake would lunge at him, coil its muscular body around him, and take him under again. Virtual or not—no air was no air and being crushed was being crushed.

Tim whispered a quick prayer.

Suddenly he heard something. A roar of some kind. Muffled by the water, it seemed to grumble up around him—a huge disturbance, the concussion surging through the water. Tim felt it. The snake felt it, too, and turned toward the new, bigger disturbance. After a moment's confusion, the snake lost interest in Tim and pulled its massive body away.

Disbelieving but greatly relieved, Tim bobbed to the surface to see Kelly peering off into the shadows. "What happened?" he called, watching the large snake swim away from them.

"A tree fell—uprooted. I was just about to dive under to see how I could help when it fell over. A monster tree—I couldn't believe the roar when it hit the water. But we can talk about that later. Let's get out of this water."

His hand stinging from where he'd been bitten, Tim only nodded. Without another word they headed for land and the flickering light beyond. Was the light coming from the trapper's cabin—the $x$ on the map—the first checkpoint?

Hammond Helbert, still inside an elf's digitized body, sat in a deserted virtual saloon in a deserted virtual western town not far from where the president, his son, and that meddlesome Morty Craft were being held hostage by the herd of frozen buffalo. On the table in front of him was displayed the virtual video. It was a small television-like screen with an equally small keyboard. By entering a character's name, he could see in primitive stick figure form what was happening to that character. He had watched what happened to Kelly and Tim, and he was fuming.

Hammond had found Tim and Kelly soon after leaving his captives. At first he had been elated that they had found their way into the Special Forces Training Area. He knew that the area was a challenge to seasoned army veterans; two kids would never make it through. But why had they veered away from his original trap in the first place?

Hammond knew that computers don't act on their own, but Virtual Reality was different. Things were created to have a certain life of their own—a limited life within parameters—but a life that allowed things to just happen to them sometimes. So he figured this was just one of those times. Something somewhere intervened to create another path just as the kids were coming through the entrance tube. He had laughed when he saw that they had been deposited in the Special Forces swamp. He knew the dangers in there because he had helped develop them. He knew those snakes were all but deadly. When he saw the snakes appear he figured that he'd get his revenge after all—get it quickly and decisively. Then that tree toppled.

At first he was just irritated by the kids' escape—now he was enraged.

Maybe it was just one of those random events. The swamp was programmed to act like a swamp—tree root systems were being eroded all the time by the water currents. When eroded enough, the trees would topple. But why did it happen at that moment—just when his snakes were about to make his day?

Now he watched the kids climb up on land. "They're not home free yet," the elf growled. "This little journey of theirs is just beginning."

Morty Craft knew that he, the president and his son were in trouble. But he knew nothing of what Tim and Kelly were up against. That worried him. He prayed and consciously gave them over to the Lord for safekeeping. But he still couldn't keep himself from worrying, for he knew who his enemy was, and he was a persistent enemy. Gar had told him—it was Hammond Helbert.

"He said we were just bait," the president said. "You must be the prize."

"He wants revenge," muttered Morty.

"Who is that guy?" the president asked.

"The brother of VR's inventor—a bad guy." Morty looked

off into the distance—toward the virtual horizon. "Where are Tim and Kelly?"

"Who?" Gar and his father asked simultaneously.

"My niece and nephew are out there in Virtual Reality someplace, and Hammond must know where—whatever revenge he's trying to extract, he'll be able to do it in spades out there."

"Revenge on kids?" The big mouse frowned. "Who takes revenge on kids?" Then he shook his head as if shaking off the thought. "All that aside," he said, "I need to get out of here. I've got a *country* to run. And this country's not something you can leave on its own for too long."

Gar said, his eyes downcast, "I didn't mean to get you into this."

"You're fourteen, and it's time to start using your head," the president growled. "Ever since your mother died you've been uncontrollable. Now you've not only done something stupid—you've put the whole country in jeopardy."

"But how could I know—"

Morty sensed the beginning of a long dispute so he tuned them out. A long dispute wouldn't get them out of there. Morty decided to spend his time formulating an escape. After a few minutes considering every possible escape route and finding them closed, he concluded there wasn't one.

More from futility than an expectation that it would work, he said, "Computer: message." Maybe Helbert had forgotten to turn off the message capability. But he hadn't. A moment later two words were displayed at the bottom right of his visor: "Facility unavailable."

Morty fell against the transparent wall and then kicked it. He didn't expect it to budge, and it didn't. He sighed. "I hope Kelly and Tim are doing better than I am," he muttered to himself.

The battle between the president and his son raged in the background, the president definitely winning. Now he grumbled about some meeting he was missing. *He has a point,* Morty thought. He was the president, and his time was valuable—very valuable. But Morty had no desire to listen to him complain. He kicked the wall again. "I'm a genius," he groaned. "I must be able to think my way out of here."

# CHAPTER 6

The trapper's cabin was little more than an organized pile of sticks. It could have been built better by a beaver. But that didn't matter. Something waited for them in there, and Tim and Kelly had to find out what it was.

Crouching cautiously by a tree not ten yards from it, Tim asked, "See anyone?"

"No."

"Well, here goes."

Both stood and stepped into the open. After a deep breath for confidence and a quick prayer, they boldly approached the cabin.

"Why, Kelly!" a voice spoke from the cabin's top step. "Is that you?" A green-clad, pointy eared elf stood in the flickering light wearing a huge grin.

"Harve?" Kelly responded, seeing her old friend. Harve was a computer character who had helped Kelly through Virtual Reality in her last adventure. She had learned to trust him. "What are you doing here?"

"Why, Harve," Tim said. "Is Barney around anywhere?" Barney was a roguish little guy with an English accent who had helped Tim in the same adventure. They, too, had become fast friends.

"You'll see him later, maybe," the little computer character said. "What brings you into this miserable place? Since they've put me here I've hated it. Snakes, alligators, rude natives—horrible place."

"We haven't been here an hour yet and we agree," Kelly told him.

"You're on duty here?" Tim queried.

"You know the army," Harve sighed. "When they ask it's an *order*. I'm the partisan—the friendly native. I provide the next bit of information. Are you two in the army now? Trying to be all you can be, eh? Four-H wasn't enough?"

"No. We're looking for Uncle Morty, who may be trapped someplace in VR with the president of the United States and his son."

"Trapped—just like me. But you know me. I can only do what I'm programmed to do. But your problem certainly *sounds* impressive."

"Do you know where the VR control room is?" Kelly asked. "We need to turn on the palm escape buttons."

"Maybe I did at one time, but not anymore. My database is quite limited nowadays."

"So you can't help us find Uncle Morty?"

Harve considered that for a moment. "No. My freedom days are over. You know the military. At least they left me with my looks." He sighed gratefully. "Now I just stay put."

Disappointed, the kids eyed each other. "Well," Tim began, "we're sort of rushed. What information do you have for us?"

Harve opened a briefcase that sat on a nearby chair. He pulled out a letter-sized envelope and another map and handed it to Kelly.

It was much like the last one, only now the path that led from the entry point to the trapper's cabin was extended. This time right to the middle of an area marked "Alligators sighted." In the same place they saw the *x* marked "control room." When Kelly adjusted the map so that the flickering lamplight illuminated the control room *x*, it began to flash as before.

"Harve, take a look at this." She held out the map to him. "Is there a better route to get to here?" She pointed to the pulsing *x*.

"Where?"

"To the *x* there. It's flashing."

Harve looked puzzled. "I don't see anything. There's nothing on the map where you're pointing."

Tim's brows furled. "Sure, there is. It's right here. You don't see that?"

"See what?"

Kelly pulled the map back. *Strange,* she thought. But there was no use asking again. Obviously Harve couldn't help.

Harve continued with his duties. "Go along the path to the Grand Banyan Tree."

"The Grand Banyan," Tim repeated. "What's there?"

"Your next set of instructions."

"Will they be pinned there or something—like those back there?"

"Just remember this—ask the one who knows."

"What's that mean?"

"How many things could it mean? Also you need to watch out for the natives. They've been sighted further south, and there is a faction among them that would prefer we leave."

"Sounds good to me," Kelly said flatly.

"Most want our help—but a small group doesn't. They are in league with the invaders and expect to come to power when the invaders are successful."

"How can we tell who's good and who's bad?"

"The ones shooting poisoned darts at you are bad. Well, that's not entirely true—if they're not shooting poisoned darts at you they could be luring you into a trap."

"Special Forces stuff gets complicated," Tim groaned.

"What about the alligators?" Kelly asked—she figured she hated alligators about as much as snakes. "The map says we're walking right into the middle of alligator country. I really don't want to do that."

"Oh, alligators, right. I'm glad you mentioned them. There was an official headquarters communication on them this morning. Here." Harve handed her another piece of paper from the briefcase.

In the flickering lamplight she saw that it was on official army stationery,

| From: | Commanding General |
| | Special Forces |
| | |
| To: | All Officers and Non-Commissioned Officers |
| | |
| Subject: | Proceeding through Alligator Infested |
| | Swamp—Protective Instructions |

*Watch your toes!*

"Watch your toes?" Kelly repeated.

"Sound advice, I'll be bound—now for your mission," Harve said calmly.

Tim replied, "We've got only one mission. Get to that control room and activate the palm buttons as quickly as possible."

"A fine objective, I'm sure. But if you ever want to get out of the swamp you have to accomplish another mission."

"If we ever want to get out?" Kelly questioned.

"You have to give this message," Harve tapped the envelope in Kelly's hand, "to the chief of the native population."

"Where's he?" Tim asked.

"Or she," Kelly added.

"He's in his regal hut—you'll know it when you see it." Harve became grave. "But if you give it to the wrong person, or if you lose it—particularly while you're watching out for those little toes of yours—you'll have to go through this training again." Harve hesitated, then gave a knowing smile. "You encountered a few of our skinnier friends in the swamp back there?"

Kelly's brows knit. "Yes?"

"Where there were three of them this time, all the dangers are multiplied by ten if you go through again. How do you think you would have done against thirty snakes?"

Tim took charge of the envelope. "I'll take care of the message," he said arrogantly and stuffed it in his fatigue shirt breast pocket.

"Good," said Kelly. "When you lose it, that will make my day."

"Okay," Harve continued, "there's just one more thing—weapons."

"How about a couple of bazookas—or a flamethrower?"

Harve laughed. "No." He pulled out a hunting knife, which Kelly promptly grabbed.

"You lost the other one," she said to Tim. "This one's mine."

"But a snake bit me—it hurt."

Harve's expression went from grave to alarmed. "A snake bit you—one of the little ones?"

"Yes, why?"

"That's serious."

"How serious?"

"Soon your vision will begin to blur, you'll experience fatigue—you'll get tired, and it will be hard to run. If you haven't gotten out of the swamp by the time things have gone completely black or you're completely worn out, you'll have to go through it again."

Kelly asked, "How long before all this happens?"

"An hour maybe," Harve said evaluatively. "But you're a skinny kid—it will probably work faster."

"If we get to the end before?" Tim asked.

"Then you're home free," Harve said. "You'd better hurry. By the way, there's a compass at the end of the knife handle." He looked off toward the horizon. "Sun's coming up—that will make things easier."

The kids followed Harve's eyes. The eastern horizon was beginning to turn pink, the light reaching tentatively into the swamp, shadows became more pronounced as did the path they would be following.

Kelly, who had learned to read maps in scouts, scanned the map again. Tim had never joined—he always said that living on a farm was like camping anyway, so who needed it. "North-northeast in a straight line," she announced. "We'd better hurry—we probably only have about forty-five minutes left until your lights go out."

"Good thinking," said Harve.

■

Terry Baker hated the situation. He hated having his boss, the president, tied up. There were things to do, people to see, legislation that needed the president's involvement. Politics was an ever-changing picture. And to send in kids and some weird genius to take care of it didn't make a lick of sense.

Maybe they would get the job done. They would at least tell the president he was needed. Surely he'd put his priorities in order and come out.

But they had been in there for nearly an hour and no one had returned. What's more, as Terry watched the black suits he became increasingly confused.

"Frank," he called to the Secret Service agent, "what do you think about this?"

"What?"

"The kids are walking, climbing, doing all sorts of things while the president, his son, and that other guy are just sitting around. Something's wrong."

Frank studied the five suits for a moment. He too had wondered what was going on but hadn't said anything. Now he tried to put his thoughts into words. "I don't know anything about this Virtual Reality thing, but if the five of them were together you'd think all five of them would be doing the same thing. Maybe the kids have been sent to check something out."

"I don't like this," Terry said flatly. "Let's bite the bullet and cut him out of there. The president might get shocked a little, but he'll live. Something's going on in there. We're talking about the security of the United States here."

Frank studied the president's aide as if deciding what the man meant. Actually he knew what he meant. Rather, he was deciding whether to reveal something he knew might change Baker's mind.

"Well," Baker continued, "what do you think?"

"Not a good idea," Frank said simply.

"Why?"

Frank remained expressionless for a long moment, then he relaxed and gave Baker an understanding smile. "Call Murphy. Suggest it to him and see what he says."

Clyde Murphy was head of the Secret Service. His primary concern was the president's safety. Baker could see him whenever he wanted.

"Murphy? Upstairs?"

"Always."

Taking another concerned look at the movement of the black suits, Baker headed upstairs.

The president was feeling increasingly panicked about his predicament, and as usual he could not let the chance to blame his son for it go by. Finally Gar could take it no more and began fighting back. When the president said that Gar's mother let him get away with everything, the battle escalated to a shouting match. The president was now roaring something about his son's lack of respect and how his irresponsibility was endangering national security. "Who will make the decision to retaliate if some terrorists decide to blow up New York!" was the last straw for Uncle Morty. Actually the last straw was seeing Gar cowering, his back pressed up against a rigid buffalo head, the president hovering over him like a menacing, mouse-shaped storm cloud.

"Mr. President," Morty finally said, interrupting the icy exchange, "with all due respect, are you two always like this?"

"Like what?" the president growled.

"Fighting."

"Are you interfering?" the president jabbed.

"Whatever you do, don't interfere," Gar snipped.

"I thought I read somewhere that you two were Christians," Morty tossed out.

"And Christian kids," the president retorted, "are to obey and respect their parents."

Gar didn't respond to his father but spoke instead to Morty. "My mom was a Christian. It was Jesus this, Jesus that all the time. Then she died in that accident—"

"River rafting," Morty said, his voice sensitive. "I read about it. Everyone did."

"Well, she said God was involved in everything," Gar went on. "When he took my mom away I couldn't understand that."

"It must have been hard. But God takes everyone sometime," Morty said. "It's hard when we love them. But she's with the Lord now. We can be happy about that."

"I guess," said the boy. "But I still miss her."

"Don't you think I do too?" his father said in accusation.

"You never loved her like I did."

"How can you say that!" his father exploded. "She was my wife."

"You never said you did. After she died you just got madder and madder at me."

"Can you blame me? You were out of control. And still are, as proved by this little mess you got me into." The president's voice was stone hard.

Morty interrupted again. "Mr. President, getting angry isn't going to help."

"It helps me," he fired back defiantly.

"You're in a situation where your power doesn't matter. Just giving an order doesn't help. We have to think our way out."

"We *have* to do something," the president bawled. "I'm in the basement of the White House, not in Beirut."

Morty only nodded. The president's last remark returned his attention to their dilemma more sharply than before. It caused his own frustration to bubble up inside and begin eating at him like acid. Where the president's power didn't seem to matter, Uncle Morty's genius didn't matter either. He'd never been in a situation like that before. Brains had always mattered. But he had to admit, they hadn't helped so far. He kicked at the invisible wall again.

After a few minutes, his resolve returned. He was a genius, and geniuses think of things. They don't give up. He had to keep thinking—sooner or later the answer would come.

The instant he said those things to himself, however, he realized how wrong he was. For his effort to be successful, the Lord had to be in on it. He decided to pray.

Tim and Kelly. What were they doing? Were they okay? Or were they facing some other menace? Morty had asked himself that question at least a hundred times—and, of course, had received no answer. He prayed again. Then he listened to father and son argue for a minute or two. More out of self-defense than anything else, he came to a conclusion—if he couldn't find a way out, maybe there was at least a way he could communicate with the outside world. Since he couldn't break out, maybe they could figure out a way to break in.

▣

Sitting in the virtual saloon, Hammond Helbert eyed the small screen. The kids had finished talking with that screwy little elf—Herb or Harve or something—and had left the first checkpoint. They were moving quickly—too quickly. They were not paying attention to the scene around them. They wanted out of that swamp as fast as they could. He couldn't blame them. And he was glad that they weren't paying attention. Any minute now they would hit the alligators, and the guys with the blow guns. They would have to pay attention then. But then it would be too late.

Hammond Helbert gave a sinister snicker.

It was here that the Special Forces trainee had been hurt. One alligator on his right leg, one on his left, both chewing and pulling—they made a wishbone out of him while the natives filled him full of darts. The guy nearly died of electric shock.

Maybe the same thing would happen to these stupid kids. It was certainly something to hope for.

回

Tim had no intention of playing this game again. With the sun rising on the horizon, he moved quickly, sloshing through the moist grass, his eyes unwaveringly ahead. Since his legs were much longer than Kelly's, he quickly outdistanced her.

"Tim, don't leave me back here," she called. "Remember the alligators."

"I'm remembering a whole bunch of things. We've got to get to the next checkpoint, find out where to go, get there, and deliver this message all in less than an hour."

"It won't help if we get separated."

Suddenly something whizzed past Kelly's ear. *Thwonk!* It lodged in a tree beside her—a thin sliver of bamboo guided by colorful feathers—a dart.

"Tim, we have company."

Tim took a quick glance around. Trees, brush, shadows. Nothing moved. He turned and started walking again. "If we keep moving we're a harder target."

Kelly didn't know whether that was true or not, but they had little choice. If they stopped, their enemy would only get closer.

The wet grass became thicker, harder to walk through. Soon they were sloshing through shallow water, then it became a little deeper.

Kelly, now at least ten yards behind Tim and beginning to get winded, called out to him. "There's a dry path off to the right. Maybe we should take that and circle around this watery part."

"The map says to go straight."

"If it's straight why did Harve give us the compass? They're always throwing army guys curves."

"Like you know."

The water was up to Tim's ankles now. He, too, was getting winded. The water resistance on each step made moving quickly almost impossible. Maybe it would be better to do as Kelly suggested.

What he saw next made the decision for him. Not twenty yards in front of him lay an alligator. Its raggedy prehistoric form reposed on a slightly raised land area—watching Tim— waiting for him. Its mouth opened revealing its jagged teeth, and it hissed. In a moment its tail serpentined, and the ugly reptile slithered from its perch into the water. It moved toward Tim.

# CHAPTER 7

**S**eeing the alligator ease into the swamp water, its eyes riveted on him, Tim spun and ran with all he was worth back to the solid ground. As he passed Kelly, Kelly reversed direction and followed. The water only to their shoe tops now, Tim asked, "Where's that path?"

"Over there." Kelly pointed anxiously. "We have to keep track of our direction so we can get back on track eventually."

"Whatever—right now let's just get away from him." Tim pointed toward the alligator swimming toward them. It reached the shallows and idled there for a while, keeping a watchful eye on its human dinner.

"There's probably more of them," warned Tim.

"No kidding. But there has to be a way through this place. It's a training area, not a prison. Come on, Tim, let's find it."

As it turned out, the path was even better than they thought it would be. The ground was hard and the path well-worn. They moved quickly, keeping track of their direction as they went.

After a few minutes, however, Tim said, "Things are getting hazy, and it's getting harder to run. The VR suit is fighting me. It's simulating the effects of the snakebite."

"Just keep going," Kelly urged.

"No other choice."

"Let me know if you need help."

The outline of the trees became less distinct as Tim's vision began to blur. Fortunately the world was becoming lighter as the sun rose, and it countered slightly his growing blindness. The growing light allowed Kelly to see something else. Shadows were moving off to the side of the path—fleeting human shadows running and dodging between the trees and brush—tracking them.

"Company again," Kelly said only loud enough for her brother to hear.

"We've made it easy for them. We're running along an open path."

Without warning a dart buzzed past Kelly, zipping just before her eyes. It struck a tree beside the path.

Another dart flashed over her head toward Tim. It missed him by inches. "We're in trouble," she cried out. Another dart and another. Each missed; each seemed closer than the last, buzzing like angry mosquitoes. Tim and Kelly hunched over to present smaller targets and ran faster. As before, Tim's longer legs took the lead, but before long, Kelly began to gain on him. "It's getting harder to run," he said breathlessly as Kelly pulled alongside him.

They heard running footsteps splashing on either side.

"They've hit water," Kelly said.

The frantic splashing became more pronounced, the water deeper, the darts fewer.

"They're falling behind," Kelly exclaimed.

"Good. I don't know how much longer . . ."

Tim didn't finish his sentence. Suddenly there came a whole volley of darts. Miraculously none found its mark. The natives appeared to be gaining. After another wave of darts, one missing Tim by less than an inch, he and Kelly left the path and ran parallel to it, dodging trees. They avoided the darts but were also forced to slow down.

And leaving the path introduced a new menace—the alligators again. They avoided the path but waited near it. The first alligator in their way caused Tim and Kelly to stop, think, and finally leap over it. At the second they slowed, then jumped over it. By the third they weren't even slowing down. By the time their most frightening challenge presented itself, they'd leaped over at least ten alligators.

They both knew they couldn't go on like this forever. Soon the natives would overtake them, or when leaping *over* one alligator they'd land *on* another. As it turned out, though, neither of these fears materialized. The path they were paralleling abruptly came to an end, and a deep, alligator-infested swamp lay dead ahead!

"Looks like I won't have to worry about going blind," Tim said, panting.

"I've got the knife—maybe we can get through the swamp," Kelly encouraged.

"You're kidding."

She hadn't been when she said it. But after looking out over the water she knew they couldn't get through that swamp. Tails undulating back and forth, their broad heads pushing through the water and leaving mysterious wakes, the alligators swarmed on the water's surface. It was alive with hundreds of them, their muscular bodies and ugly, deadly heads everywhere.

Hammond Helbert laughed. Finally these kids had reached the end of their ropes. Inattention had kept them from seeing the right path a while back, and now they were about be paid back for beating him the last time. On his screen the alligators appeared as short squiggly lines. Swarms of them were waiting for four scrawny legs to enter the water.

On the path behind Tim and Kelly were the warriors, a pack of them closing fast. This would be just like the Special Forces victim who was torn apart by alligators while becoming a pin cushion. Hammond Helbert laughed again—he loved what was happening—absolutely loved it.

But then something curious occurred.

The swarms of squiggly, squirming lines—the alligators—froze. All movement stopped. The pack of natives continued to close in on the kids, but the alligators stopped writhing in the swamp. "What happened?" Hammond Helbert screamed. *What happened?*

Tim and Kelly gasped in disbelief.

The lake had turned to stone. Like lava that has suddenly cooled, what once had been black water boiling with hungry alligators was now a solid sheet that resembled black rock. The alligators' legs, bellies, and lower portions of their tales were frozen within it—but their heads and snapping, hissing jaws were still free.

Surprised and cautious, Tim placed a toe on the water. "It's hard—like glass," he announced.

"We can walk on it?" Kelly asked.

"What say we run on it?" Tim said, looking back toward the approaching natives. Another swarm of darts came toward them. Deftly they sidestepped the onslaught and hid behind a tree. The darts stuck in the hides of alligators or bounced harmlessly off the lake. Kelly and Tim emerged from the trees and stepped onto the solid water. Cautious at first, their confidence quickly ballooned and they ran.

"It seems almost sacrilegious to run on water," Kelly quipped.

It was a strange path. The solid water was a little slippery, but their rubber-soled shoes gave them some traction. The living alligators whipped their broad snouts around and snapped at their heels as they scrambled by. Even though they had to cover as much ground as they could, Kelly found herself teasing the alligators—running as close to the snapping jaws as she could without being caught. The fun ended after only a few minutes though. She leaped over one alligator, tripped on another, and fell headlong onto the water. Sliding out of control she came to rest three inches from the nose of a very ferocious, very hungry, extremely ugly one. The reptile gasped with gleeful excitement; opening its mouth wide, it lunged at her. Kelly thanked God when the frozen lake held it tight. She screamed as the jagged teeth slapped shut an inch from her nose. Scrambling backward on hands and knees, she sprang to her feet.

Her heart beating again, she picked up speed but nearly tripped over another hideous reptile. Slowing, she took a moment to regain her balance before deciding on a safer pace.

Tim, on the other hand, ran cautiously. The images were blurred, and, more often than not, he slowed to a near walk as he danced between the snapping jaws.

The natives reached the end of the path. Although they looked surprised when they encountered the solid water and the alligators imprisoned in it, they immediately followed the kids. They whooped and cried terrifyingly.

"They're gaining on us," Kelly called out.

"The alligators are really fuzzy. I hate fuzzy alligators," Tim cried.

"You want me to lead the way?"

"Just stay close."

Kelly eased up and fell in beside him.

Although running became increasingly difficult for Tim as the simulated effects of the snakebite intensified, a wave of relief broke over him as he heard Kelly announce, "I see the shore!"

In her excitement, Kelly stepped dangerously close to a snapping jaw. It lunged and tore the cuff of her pants. She stumbled but recovered quickly. "That was close."

But so was the lake's shoreline.

After a couple more steps, Kelly leaped onto the grassy edge and pulled her brother up behind her. Finding another well-worn path, Kelly made sure Tim was safely on it before letting go of him.

From behind came a sudden explosion of sound. They heard splashing and wild cries. Tim and Kelly spun and saw that the solid water had turned to wet water again, and their screaming attackers were hip deep in it, battling and swimming away from the attacking alligators.

"Virtual alligators attacking virtual natives," Tim observed, squinting to see as much as he could, a sigh of relief and exhaustion escaping from his lips. "At least they're not attacking *real* us."

"It's like the Red Sea when Moses parted it. The Israelites crossed safely, then the Egyptians drowned in it."

Tim nodded, listening to the water thrash with the battle. "We'd better get out of here—my vision is getting worse."

They turned to continue along the path but only ran a few feet. Rounding a bend in the path they stopped. With the sound of battling natives and alligators being replaced by a riot of birds, crickets, owls, and the rustle of trees, they hadn't heard what now greeted them as they stood before it.

Chaos!

Surrounding, climbing on, and hanging from a huge tree were a number of people and animals, and they all jabbered, sang, shouted, and squealed. The tree was huge. The trunk looked like a massive bundle of boa constrictors dropping from a storm of limbs, vines, and heart-shaped leaves. On the soggy ground, the roots twisted away from the bunch in all directions and buried themselves in the earth. Men and women in army fatigue uniforms, and others in civilian shirts and jeans, joined kids in jeans, shorts, and colorful tops in climbing and sliding all over the tree. One authoritative-looking fellow in a suit that also looked a little like a uniform actually sat at a desk, the desk and chair suspended from the tree by shiny steel cables.

Monkeys and children also climbed and slid down thinner trunks that dropped from limbs every ten feet or so. These new stakes in the ground helped hold up the wide canopy as well as provided new play opportunities for the kids and monkeys. From heart-shaped leaves hung cherry-like scarlet fruit that everyone picked and occasionally tossed at one another.

"This is too weird!" Kelly watched the goings-on with the frustration of a person who needed less chaos and more order.

"If it's even half of what I can see," Tim said in awe, "it's too much."

"Hey, down there," a voice called from the tree. "We're havin' fun. Wanna have some with us?"

"No time," Kelly called back to the tree. Under her breath she said, "No way."

"Do you have business to conduct?" the man at the desk asked. "I've been hanging around all day waiting for you."

"I'll bet you have," Kelly called back.

"Kelly," Tim said to his sister in a forced whisper. "That's a banyan tree."

"So?"

"It's what we're supposed to look for."

"Really?" Kelly said watching a man with lieutenant's bars do a somersault from a branch to the ground. "We're supposed to get information from them?"

"We're supposed to ask the one who knows—that's what Harve said. 'Ask the one who knows.'"

Kelly again scanned the strange scene. "Nobody here could possibly know anything."

Another military type, a woman this time, leaped from root to root around the tree, a couple of kids following. All three were yelling, the kids with high-pitched squeals.

"Are you guys going to just stand there?" a young girl chided as she stood, hands on her hips.

Kelly didn't reply to the girl. Instead she cried out to all who could hear her, "Okay, who of you knows?"

"We all know," someone cried back.

"Sure—we're all smart people," another called out. "Most of us know everything worth knowing."

"Then where do we go next?" Kelly asked.

"Who are you?"

"Go where next?"

"It really depends."

For Tim the chaos was just a blur, the antics of the people only fleeting, jumbled shadows. His frustration was nearing the boiling point. "This isn't getting us anywhere," he said.

"Ask the one who knows," Kelly repeated, again searching the faces of the people—even the animals. Some of the monkeys looked more responsible than most of the people. "Lord, we need your help."

Kelly wasn't sure how she heard it, but she did—the sounds of brush being pushed aside and a person emerging from it. A girl, maybe eight or ten years old, wearing long pants and flannel shirt that were unusual for the heat. Her eyes looked sharply left and right. Her expression, though smudged with dirt and sweat, remained cool even when she glanced at the tree and those bouncing around it.

"You see something?" Tim asked, noticing Kelly's silent intensity.

"Just a sec," Kelly said and stepped over to the girl.

As Kelly approached, the child stiffened, her eyes glued on Kelly's.

"Hi," greeted Kelly.

"I didn't do anything," the ten year old said defensively.

"You live in the swamp?"

"Sure. What of it?"

"You know a lot about what goes on in the swamp?"

"Some."

"Do you know where we're to go next and what we're supposed to do?"

"Who are you?"

Kelly was about to introduce herself as she would in the real world. But she caught herself. "I'm a Special Forces trainee."

The girl's expression remained the same—defensive and wary. After a moment she reached into her back pocket and retrieved an envelope. "This is probably yours then."

Kelly took the envelope. "Thank you," she said gratefully.

"Gotta go," the girl said. "See ya."

"Right," Kelly said. Without a moment's hesitation she ripped the envelope open. "It's the map we want," she called back to Tim. When she returned to his side, she studied it quickly. "The path is a straight shot to the edge of the swamp— easy sailing. The natives and the alligators are busy back there, and the only thing marked is the last checkpoint. It says 'the chief.'"

"We'd better get going," Tim urged. "A straight shot, eh? Great. Then we're on to the VR control room and then out of here. There are times when VR is less fun than other times."

Kelly looked back but the girl was gone. "I should have asked her what lay ahead—if there was anything we had to worry about."

"This is VR," Tim said with grim resolve. "There's always something to worry about."

# CHAPTER 8

"This is too easy," Kelly commented. The path was straight and flat, the trees less imposing, and the canopy of limbs, leaves, and moss less tangled letting more sunlight through. "Understand—I'm not complaining."

"I wouldn't survive anything harder," Tim said, his voice strained. "It's almost impossible to run—maybe I *have* been poisoned." They stopped frequently to rest but were still making good time.

"We'll be out of here soon," Kelly encouraged. "Then we'll find that control room."

"It's getting darker. Like a fog," Tim said.

"Keep going. It can't be much farther."

Sitting in the virtual western town, staring into his small terminal display, Hammond Helbert was beside himself. He was more than angry. He was volcanic, his rage like lava spewing everywhere. What had happened? Twice something had saved those kids. Twice now the kids had been inches from paying the proper price for beating him, and twice they had come through unscathed.

What—but the more important question—*why* had this happened?

Was it just Virtual Reality being itself? Was it some random number generator suddenly generating the magic number at the magic time causing things to happen at just the right moment to help these stupid kids? Was it pure chance?

No. The odds were too great. Something he didn't understand had to be going on. Whatever it was, it was beating him again.

And he hated being beaten. His brother had beaten him

throughout his life, and he had no intention of letting anyone else do that to him.

His rage grew, boiled, and finally erupted.

They had only one test left to overcome before leaving the swamp, and if something miraculous occurred to get them through it, Hammond Helbert would act. He had helped program these training areas within VR to reward failure with severe and lasting pain. He had no intention of letting those kids out unscathed.

Hammond Helbert laughed. "Am I ever looking forward to that!"

◻

"How's it going?" Kelly asked Tim. He had been slowing, his steps labored and irregular, like a jogger running out of muscle—then he staggered and nearly fell. When he stumbled, she grabbed him by the arm and helped steady him.

"It feels like I'm running straight uphill. But that's not the real problem—the lights are nearly gone. I probably have only a few minutes left. How much farther do you think?"

Kelly, too, was getting fatigued as she doggedly planted one foot before the other. She hadn't speculated about how much farther. The end would come when it came. But now that Tim expressed real concern, she straightened and peered off into the distance.

"I see something out there," she exclaimed joyfully. "It looks like a large jungle hut—a castle almost."

Large, grass-covered domes, misty in the distance, reached above the vegetation. It had to be where the chief lived. They'd give him the message in the envelope and be out of there.

"It's a piece of cake," Kelly encouraged him. "Just hang on."

Just then everything changed. As they came over a small rise, Kelly cried, "Tim, stop!" She grabbed his arm to hold him back.

"What—oh, no. What's out there? It's all so blurred and dark. What is it?"

Kelly knew exactly how to describe it—she just didn't want to. They had stopped running about a foot before a sheer cliff—actually, it was one edge of a steep canyon that stretched forever in both directions. It was about twenty yards across and another twenty deep. But it wasn't the fall that would cause trouble, it was what waited at the bottom—a sea of more angry, hungry alligators. They lay entwined together like a living, hissing carpet, waiting not too patiently for their next meal.

There was a way across, but Kelly wasn't happy about it. A single log spanned the canyon. It was only wide enough for one person at a time—maybe only strong enough for that one person, as well.

"What is it?" Tim asked anxiously again.

"We have a problem." Kelly described the canyon and the log across it.

"You're actually pretty good walking things like that," Tim said hopefully. "You took tumbling, right? Maybe you ought to just go ahead and leave me here. If you get to the VR control room fast, maybe I'll only have to go through half of this again."

Kelly shook her head. "If we crawl on our bellies, grabbing the log with our arms and knees, we'll spread our weight out so you won't have to see anything."

Tim went first so Kelly could watch him. He inched his body out onto the log and began to crawl. Kelly did the same. They were both on the log, both peering down at the sea of wriggling, hissing reptiles, each knowing what would happen if they made a mistake. After a few minutes of progress their spirits rose.

Too soon. The log groaned and began to make splintering sounds.

"One banana split too many," Kelly said. "You go ahead. I'll go back and wait on the other side."

Tim only nodded. He knew he desperately needed to get that message in his pocket delivered. There was no time to do anything but move forward. He worked his legs, his arms. He hugged the log so that he felt every contour. It shuddered now and then. But nothing stopped him or slowed him down.

"You're about two-thirds of the way," he heard Kelly call from the opposite bank where she now stood.

He continued to crawl inch by inch, movement by agonizing movement. He tried to tell himself that it was all unreal—all just the ravings of a computer. Yet the scraping on his knees, stomach, and hands was real—the pain was real. As was the world going slowly black. Most real of all was the knowledge that if he didn't get the message delivered in time he would have to do this all over again with ten times the danger and the pain.

He heard a sudden cracking sound and felt a frightening sensation that the log was giving way. He had to be nearing the end, but whoever programmed this training area was determined to scare him to death; the cracking sound became more pronounced. He scrambled faster.

The cracking sound intensified as did the feeling that the log was giving way.

Faster. His ankles and knees scraped with pain. But he didn't give up. He couldn't give up. He prayed and reached out for more log—and touched land! A clump of grass!

The cracking became the sound of splintering wood.

Tim grabbed what felt like a vine. It held him as he pulled himself off the log. The instant he was safely on the other side, the log splintered, both ends falling into the canyon—Kelly was trapped on the other side.

"Are you okay?" she called out to him.

"It's getting real dark. How are you going to get across?"

"Don't worry about me. I'll figure something out. You get to the chief. You don't have much time. Find that control room and get us out of here."

Tim knew she was right. She was powerless for now, and he was their only chance to complete the mission.

"I'll be praying for you," Tim called back to her.

"I'll be praying for you too. Now get going!"

Straining to see anything, he turned and began to grope forward. But all the eyestrain in the world wouldn't help now. The shadows were hardly distinguishable from one another. To find and follow a path would be all but impossible.

He was about to give up when he felt a small hand in his.

A child's hand.

Tim could hardly make the little person out, but there was the dimmest of outlines—a young child.

"Come with me," the child said softly.

Tim, feeling a wave of relief, did just that.

Kelly saw her brother being led away. She hoped that was a good thing, but whether it was or wasn't, it didn't change her situation any—she had a real problem. If she were going to follow her brother, she had to get across that canyon.

She ran down the edge of it in both directions and found nothing. Unwilling to believe she was totally stranded, she ran up and down it again and again found nothing.

Standing where the log had once spanned the canyon, she thought. If she had an axe she could cut down one of the trees so that it fell across the canyon. A falling tree had saved them once before; it could save her again. But she didn't have an axe.

She did have the knife—but cutting a tree down with a knife might be a little tough.

She felt a drop of rain. Then another.

She looked up at the sky. While she was worrying about getting across the canyon, dark, threatening clouds had formed.

More drops. Within seconds, the rain was falling in gray sheets. Virtual Reality could not simulate the feeling of being wet, but it simulated the avalanche of water splattering down upon Kelly all too well. After only a few moments she became oppressed by it.

Then she felt the wind—great gusts of it that drove her off balance. To avoid being blown into the canyon, she backed away from it.

Above the rush of rain came a thunderous roar from the base of the canyon. Carefully approaching it, Kelly peered down. Her heart leaped. The alligators had been swept away by a boiling river of water—run off from the storm. Maybe the storm would end, and she would be able to cross when the river subsided.

But that could take forever, and Tim had already disappeared down the path. She hoped the child was leading him to the chief. A disquieting thought struck her. Why would a child be programmed into a U.S. Army Special Forces training area? Wouldn't Tim be just left to go blind and start the training exercise over? It didn't make sense.

Another gust of wind. This one battered her and nearly drove her over the edge. She stepped back from the cliff.

Thunder exploded overhead. Lightning flashed, tearing the sky in jagged brilliance. The wind blew the trees wildly, stripping them of leaves, tearing off branches, whipping them into a frenzy. Thunder blasted. Lightning flashed like a divine lance.

A tree burst into flames but was immediately extinguished by the rain.

Kelly pulled her fatigue jacket tightly around her to ward off the onslaught.

More lightning. This struck nearby, so close that she felt the ground shudder. She turned away, frightened by the intensity of it, nearly bursting into tears when she heard wood being ripped and split.

She darted farther into the trees and crouched frightened behind one.

But she stayed there only a second—a thick tree trunk had been toppled by the lightning and now spanned the canyon! With the blistering wind and lightning, there was no telling how long it would remain. Gathering all her courage and saying another prayer, this one more pleading than any before, Kelly launched herself toward the newly made bridge. Reaching it, she leaped onto the trunk. Grabbing protruding limb after limb to steady herself, she quickly made it to the other side. The moment she stepped on land again, another rage of lightning struck the trunk at its midpoint and split it like kindling. It fell into the boiling river below.

Her heart thundered in her chest as she turned toward the chief's hut—or what she hoped was his hut—and ran.

□

Hammond Helbert's fist came down on the table with such force that it shattered. He couldn't remember ever being so angry, frustrated, and confused.

"Lightning?! A child?!" he cried. "There are no children in the swamp."

Yet he knew that the virtual natives were capable of having virtual families. There were earlier versions of the programs that had the trainees being helped by families. He had squashed all of those in favor of something more dangerous—even lethal. Maybe some of that old programming still existed. Maybe children had come about.

"But why are they helping these two kids? This can't be chance. It just can't be!"

He rubbed his chin, then drove his hands over his hair, then rubbed his hands together. It was too late to do anything to those kids in the swamp. They would be out of there in a minute or two.

But there was a lot he could do to them when they left it. The only active exit would drop them right into this little western town. Now *that* was something he could live with.

◙

The rain stopped as quickly as it had started, and when Kelly found the chief's hut, or what appeared to be the chief's hut, she found it deserted—no sign of Tim or the child. He must have gone on ahead—which was good for him but not so good for her. Without the message to give to the chief, she wasn't sure how she would be treated.

The hut was every bit as big as it appeared to be on the outside. But it was an expansive, empty room. She saw a spiral staircase in the back—a curious thing to have in a hut.

She crossed to it quickly and began to climb. About halfway up she heard music. Softly at first, growing as she mounted the stairs—it was a skillful Spanish guitar strumming melodically. When she finally stepped off the stairs, she was confronted with a picture she could hardly believe.

Tim reclined on a grassy lounge; two lovely ladies, each in a flowered sarong, fanned him with huge palm leaves while he rested contentedly, eyes closed.

"Why aren't you gone?" Kelly cried.

Eyes popping wide, Tim rose with a start. "Kelly," he sputtered. "Great! I knew you'd figure it out. The chief—where is the chief, anyway?—anyway, the chief suggested that I wait here. I was beat. I knew I couldn't go much farther, so I thought I'd give you a few minutes."

"Right. You just didn't want to leave *them*."

With sheepish eyes glancing back and forth between the sarongs, he smiled. "That was part of it."

"How do we get out of here?"

His sight completely recovered now, his muscles rested, Tim got to his feet and pointed to a door at the far end of the upper room. "Through there."

"Then let's go. Hopefully, the VR control room is just beyond it."

"Okay." Tim turned to each of the women. "Sorry, ladies,

but duty calls." Then he turned to Kelly. "How'd you do it anyway?"

"What do you care? Why didn't you come back for me?"

"The chief gave me only two choices. Stay here and wait or leave the swamp area altogether. I couldn't go help."

"Well, you sure were relaxed about it all."

"Tired—just tired. Come on. If we're going, let's go."

Tim led the way to the door, and they opened it.

"I don't think I like this," Kelly said as she peered out into nothingness.

"We're just supposed to step off."

But it was a long, very long drop. Except for the cliff that stretched in either direction disappearing in the distance, they could see nothing out there but mist.

"If flying scares me, dropping really scares me."

"There's no choice," Tim said.

Kelly swallowed hard. "Well, things are seldom what they seem."

Tim gave her hand an encouraging squeeze and placed his toes on the edge of the world. "Well, here goes." He stepped off.

Kelly saw him drop like a rock into the mist below her. One more deep breath to force her heart back down into her chest, and she stepped off right behind him.

# CHAPTER 9

**T**erry Baker returned to the Virtual Reality room in the basement of the White House and approached Frank Holloway. The energy that characterized him seemed to have evaporated.

"Why wasn't I told about the president's heart condition before?" he asked the Secret Service agent.

"The president's orders—only those responsible for his safety could know. Now you understand why we can't risk those electric storage cells in his black suit firing off and sending a charge through him. There's a good chance his heart wouldn't take it."

"How long has he known?"

"A couple of years."

"Why didn't he tell me?"

"Doesn't matter now. We can't cut him out of there. We just have to hope the Crafts will get him out."

Terry turned defeatedly toward the black suits. "Why are the president, his son, and that Morty guy standing around doing nothing while those two kids are so active?"

"Don't know. Don't know anything about that stuff."

Baker looked at his watch. "They've been in there almost an hour now. They haven't even sent us a message. That's too long. Something's wrong."

Frank looked off toward the other agents. "No luck getting a hold of Matthew Helbert," he said. "We sent a local guy out to his place. He didn't find him."

Baker nodded.

"I think you'd better confer with the vice president," Frank suggested.

Baker said nothing for a long moment then shook his head. "If the opposition found out that the president is locked up in Virtual Reality instead of doing his job, our entire political party will be down the drain. And they'll find out if the vice president starts filling in for the president. No. We don't do that until we're absolutely compelled to. And maybe not even then." Baker eyed the kids' black suits again. "Now they look like they're floating or something. They don't have time to float. They're there to do a job. Not to play around floating!"

◫

Tim had never seen anything like it. Never. It took his breath away. The universe spread before him—all of it—the wash of the Milky Way, the sprinkles of stars and galaxies above and below it—blazing speckles on black velvet that went on forever. Planted in the middle of it was the sterile glow of the moon, its craters visible, various sized pockmarks, the legacy of a thousand celestial encounters. The earth loomed below—its vast expanse a blue-green sphere, waiting expectantly, eager to take them back. He and Kelly spun weightlessly—he in awe over what he saw, she frantic.

"It's something else," Tim declared, his voice a thin, electronic crackling in Kelly's space helmet.

But she didn't hear it. She didn't care about what he said. Flying was bad enough *with* a plane—flying without a plane was excruciating. Falling thirty thousand feet was one thing—falling more than two hundred miles was quite another. The instant Kelly managed the breath it took, she screamed.

"You okay?"

She gasped for more breath, her heart like lead in the middle of her stomach. "You're kidding, right?" she exclaimed. "I'm afraid to move. I could accidentally cut the string holding me up."

"There's no gravity—you can't fall."

"I can always fall." With paralyzed eyes she watched her brother. He wore a bulky white space suit, his head encased in a large white helmet, his back carrying a boxy air pack, the United States flag on his shoulder. He floated effortlessly, holding a T-shaped mechanism in his hand. She couldn't see her own suit, but it was undoubtedly the same. She hoped it was cushioned so when she hit ground she'd bounce. She held the same mechanism but hardly knew it was there.

"Look," Tim summoned her attention. He pushed a button

on the mechanism, and one of the crosspieces ignited and pushed him in the opposite direction. "The right button sends you left, the left one sends you right; push both and you go forward. It's got little rockets in it or something."

"I'm not pushing anything—I'm not moving."

Tim shook his head in frustration, but, using his T, he eased alongside her. "Grab my belt and I'll tow you."

"To where?" she asked, her voice strained.

"To there." He pointed upward.

Kelly looked. Then gasped.

"There's nothing like this in Wisconsin," she exclaimed.

Above them, spinning slowly, as big as a skyscraper floating on its side, was the space station. It was a massive structure. It had two mammoth wheels with spokes reaching to the center axle. The axle connected the two wheels at their center. In bold red and blue letters, across the full length of it, were the words *United States of America—Freedom IV*. Six other tubes, each spaced at equal intervals, reached from wheel to wheel. At the midpoint of the axle was another structure built perpendicular to it. It had a bubble-shaped topknot—an observation tower. Extending out from the wheels were several huge, rectangular black wings.

"Those are solar panels producing the station's power," Tim offered. "I read about *Freedom I*. It was a lot smaller than this one. NASA must be looking ahead."

"That's fine, but my nerves can't take it much longer out here. How do we get in?" Kelly asked.

"Don't know," Tim admitted. "Let's get closer and find a door. This is like 'Star Trek.'"

"The one thing it is not like is solid ground," Kelly said, still falling short in her fight with her fears. Another quick prayer. Nothing changed, but at least she didn't feel quite so alone. "I got up this morning thinking the most excitement I'd have was seeing Bernie—"

"This beats Bernie all over the place."

Kelly suddenly remembered the almost kiss. Had her time with Bernie really only happened that morning?

"Look!" she pointed. "A door."

It was a rectangular air lock on the edge of the right wheel.

Tim aimed himself toward it dragging Kelly along. They pushed a button by the door. The door *whoosh*ed open, and they floated into a ten-by-ten room. The instant they cleared the opening, the door *whoosh*ed shut, and they heard the hiss of air filling it. After a minute or two a red light flashed—"Safe."

Each felt around for the virtual helmet release, found it, and soon they were out of their space suits. They now wore sleek, form fitting jumpsuits—blue with a red lightning bolt across the chest.

"Even the outfits look like 'Star Trek,'" Tim commented.

A man's voice with the tenor of an instructor filled the room. "Welcome to *Freedom Four*, the first community-based space station. *Freedom Four* is in geosynchronous orbit two hundred twenty nautical miles above the earth's surface. Although *Freedom Four* is designed for permanent habitation, for this training exercise, you are the only ones aboard the station and are responsible for carrying out any and all assignments directed your way. Draw upon your training in Houston and you'll do fine. Again, welcome aboard and have a good session."

"Maybe we should transfer back to Houston for a refresher," Tim quipped.

"Failing that, what now?" Kelly asked as if her brother might know.

"Let's go look around," Tim suggested. "Sounds like something will happen."

"All we need—more happening."

Hammond Helbert growled at the small monitor screen. The fire burned so hot within him that it turned everything to energy—hot, purposeful energy. Those kids were supposed to come to his little western town where he could trample them with a million tons of rampaging buffalo. "Is that too much to ask?" he called to the gods of VR—those million and one little random number generators that made things behave, in his mind at least, like true reality.

But those hapless gods didn't answer. When he realized that he was actually calling to someone in VR, someone who had to be manipulating VR for the kids' benefit, he hesitated, took a deep breath of understanding, and whispered what he had probably known all along.

"Matthew is in here," he groaned, poisonous ties lashing every word together. Hammond hated his younger brother. He'd hated him all his life but never as much as today. He thought he hated Matthew when their very rich grandmother took Matthew on a six-month cruise around the world when Matthew was ten and Hammond was twelve. She left Hammond behind because he had set fire to her cat's tail. He thought he hated Matthew when their father chose to spend his meager savings on tutors for Matthew so that he could go to MIT when he was still a young teen just because Hammond had started that fire in the school science lab—the teacher had given him an unfair grade—the teacher was against him too. And he really thought he hated Matthew when his grandmother left everything to him. That money allowed Matthew to build the Virtual Reality machine.

But now that Matthew had gotten religion and was messing up Hammond's opportunity to work his revenge, Hammond hated him more than ever.

He wouldn't let Matthew get away with it.

Hammond suddenly smiled—a leering, triumphant smile. Beating his brother would make revenge even sweeter. It would make winning beyond wonderful, beyond magnificent—winning would be *mind blowing*.

An idea exploded in his brain. So, that's how Matthew was intervening on those kids' behalf.

He wasn't changing the programming. To do that he would have to write new programs, recompile them, stop the Virtual Reality machine, and start it again. That wasn't happening. But Matthew could easily change specific characteristics. He could make water like stone instead of "watery," make tree roots ready to give way, open up areas within VR. Every object in VR had a place where its characteristics were defined. Matthew could simply display that area for any object he wanted and change its characteristics. Then the next time a VR program used the object—tree, water, area—it would be different; the water would be hard, the tree would fall, the area—like the Special

Forces camp or the NASA space station—would be open and ready for business.

Simple.

To verify his theory, Hammond entered the command to display the names of all VR visitors. Six names appeared—*who's Mickey Mouse? Oh, right, the president. No Matthew ... But Matthew could rig it so he doesn't show up. Yes—Matthew has to be in here.* It couldn't be just chance at work. Characteristics don't change by chance—they have to be changed by someone who knows how. If he, Hammond, could get in, so could Matthew. And if he turned the switch to lock Matthew out, he'd lock himself out as well. There was no choice but to beat Matthew at his own game.

*Well,* Hammond Helbert thought, *if Matthew can be their guardian angel—I can be their Destroying Angel—their devil.* "We all need a devil—and I'll be a beaut." He thought for a moment. An idea came alive—a brilliant idea. "I wonder what it's like to be drilled by a meteor? I'll bet it smarts." Hammond quickly struck a few keys. A skeletal display of the space station appeared in the lower left corner of the screen. "There's got to be a meteor or two spinning around that I can use. Ah—there. Now to send it forward." He entered a few quick keystrokes. A long string of numbers appeared at the bottom of his screen— the orbital formula—a mix to speed, direction, the gravitational pull of the sun, moon, and earth and maybe other things—all laid out before him. He knew a little about such calculations, and he could use his instinct to fill in the gaps of what he didn't know. "Well," he said, scratching his virtual, elfin head, "here goes. You ready Matthew? This should be good."

回

The air lock was on the edge of the right wheel. Now Tim and Kelly walked along the inside—a tube with an arching roof and flat floor. Their boots stuck slightly to the floor—magnetic boots or maybe the result of centrifugal force—Tim explained to his sister.

"Like you know," she chided.

"I do know—I've seen all the 'Star Treks' and the movies twice."

"Then you won't have to go to college at all."

Tim didn't reply but kept his eyes ahead looking for something that would help them out of "NASA-land" and on to the VR control room. He was still wondering why they hadn't ended up near it when they left the swamp.

"I hear something," Kelly announced.

Tim did too. Chirping and grunting sounds coming from up ahead. Moments later they saw a blinking blue sign—"Menagerie." Below it was a series of gauges set against the arching wall.

"A zoo," Kelly exclaimed and ran to it.

Tim followed and stood beside her in front of three iron cages. Inside them were different species of monkeys—a gibbon which, according to the small plaque outside its cage, was really a small ape; a spider monkey with long legs, arms, and tail; and a large, goofy-looking orangutan. Each had a habitat in which it lived and played. The two smaller monkeys bounced around their habitats as if they were avoiding hot spots—from rock to limb to tire and back again. The orangutan, on the other hand, reclined on a thick mat. Above such shenanigans, it sat contorting its immense lips to form new and thrilling faces.

Beside the cages, hanging on a hook, was a large iron key.

"Why do you think they're here?" Kelly asked.

"Experiments maybe. You don't think they'll want us to do anything with the orangutan? I'm really not in the mood."

Kelly stepped over to the gibbon's cage. Maybe a yard tall, it nimbly swung back and forth on a limb with one hand while scratching its side with the other.

"Look over there," Tim interrupted.

Alongside the cages was an electronic poster. The heading pulsed: "Trainee Instructions."

It read: "This is an event-driven exercise. Perform all tasks as they are presented, following appropriate instructions as you do."

Tim grunted, "That sounds straightforward enough."

"And we don't have to do anything with *them*," Kelly said, indicating the monkeys.

Then something slowly, magically appeared beside the instructions.

"A map—like in the swamp!" Kelly exclaimed.

It was clearly a diagram of the space station. Listed on the side, with lines pointing to them, were a number of areas: living quarters, farming areas with the various crops, animal sections, machinery storage and maintenance blocks, administrative offices, schools, laboratories. The lists went on and on and represented the entire space station. The domed building at the midpoint of the central axle was the bridge.

"That must be where the captain works," Tim told Kelly.

"Ol' Spock and his pointy ears."

"Kirk was captain," Tim pointed out with a note of condescension. "Spock was science officer."

"Look here," Kelly said, pointing to another marker near the *You are here* dot. "Further Instructions," it read and indicated an exercise room.

"Exercise!" Kelly exclaimed. "I had enough of that in the swamp."

Tim studied the map more closely. "Do you see any way to bypass all this and get to the control room?"

"Funny you should ask," Kelly said, pointing. In the lower right corner, just where it had appeared on the swamp map, was the same $x$ and the words "control room." As before, it was flashing softly.

"I guess we'd better get going," Tim urged. "The sooner we make things happen, the sooner we find the control room."

"We said the same thing in the swamp—now we're here."

"Hopefully, we're closer than before," Tim said.

"Well, stay close. Your legs move faster than mine, and we don't want to be separated. Who knows what this place is like."

Tim only nodded.

Kelly turned back to the monkeys. "See you guys."

To her surprise they chirped and grunted in reply, and the orangutan twisted its lips up into a kind of smile.

They did move quickly. Being nearly weightless, they seemed to multiply their energy. The VR suits actually moved for them. Now and then they lifted totally off the floor, their steps big and quick.

"This is fun." Tim laughed as he took a chance and dove forward as if trying to take off. He actually did—like Peter Pan—arms outstretched, feet together. He finally came down, landing with a brief skid on his chest.

"You okay?"

"You try it," Tim said, getting to his feet. "I'll do better next time. I just got a little confused."

"Come on, Tim. There's no time to play around."

Tim groaned guiltily, but then brightened. "Remember, we only *think* Uncle Morty's in trouble."

Kelly shook her head. "He's in trouble. I know it. We *have* to get to that control room and activate the palm button escape. And if he's not, what does it hurt that we hurried?"

"Right," Tim said simply as they continued running.

After a few minutes, Kelly asked, "Do you think we'll ever be able to do these kinds of things for real?"

"Running in a space station?"

"Well, maybe not exactly this, but things—Exciting things, out of the ordinary things."

"Things that don't involve cows—"

"And dirt and seeds and praying for rain."

"Jesus says we'll live life to the full," Tim said.

"Will it be a real life—or like this—a virtual life?"

"Maybe it doesn't matter."

Kelly thought for a while then said, "It matters. Look at Dad. He gets up at five every morning, works on the farm all day long, and goes to bed about ten every night. Excitement for him is watching the corn grow."

"Have you seen him at around sunup when the stalks are just poking up? He *is* excited."

"I could never live a life where I have to be excited about corn." Kelly felt a sudden stab of despair.

Tim took a long look around—at the white tubular walls of the space station, the black eternity of the universe beyond. "You're not now," he said.

回

Terry Baker sat on as comfortable a chair as the security staff could find. He had been sitting there for what seemed like forever but was actually about a half hour. Frank Holloway stood. *He always stands,* Terry thought. *The guy must have cement feet.*

Terry closed his eyes for a moment—to let the world go by—but maybe he actually slept for a while. He wasn't sure. It didn't matter. When his eyes popped open, though, something was happening. "Frank."

"Huh, what?" Frank was standing near the wall looking at a magazine.

"The uncle. It looks like he's signaling or something."

Frank straightened and turned.

Morty was waving as if to get their attention. He flailed his arms for a moment, turned and flailed them some more, then turned again.

"Is he talking to us or someone inside?" Terry asked Frank.

Frank shrugged but kept his eyes glued on Morty's hands. "It looks like he's writing something with his finger."

Terry stepped closer. If Morty were writing something he was using big, exaggerated letters.

"Can you make it out?" Frank asked.

"A word? Letters? What do you think that one is?"

"An *m*," Frank speculated, "another *m,* an *o,* that was easy—another *m*—"

"An *n*," Terry corrected. "And a *d—m-m-o-n-d.*"

"An *h*—that's an *h*. He started with one of those too. *E*—was that an *e* or a *b?* That's an *l* and that's a *b,* the other thing must be an *e* and another *e.* Are you writing this down? What's that? What's that thing?" Frank was becoming excited.

"An *r.*"

"Okay, an *r.* And a *t.* What's he doing now—a point—ah—a period. It's over. He's starting again. That *h* again and it's like the *r.* I guess it's an *a.*"

"H-a-m-m-o-n-d h-e-l-b-e-r-t," Terry spelled it out. "Hammond Helbert."

"Who's that?" Frank asked.

"He's telling us more."

This time it went faster. "H-e—i-s—h-o-l-d-i-n-g—u-s—c-a-p-t-i-v-e—h-e—i-s—i-n—h-e-r-e—Period. He's starting again." Frank gnawed his lower lip. "That makes it official. The president and his son are prisoners in there." His mind still trying to come to grips with it all, he stepped over to Morty. Dodging his waving arms he tapped him on the chest. Morty stopped and gave Frank a wave of recognition.

"So what are you going to do?" Terry said, his words a challenge.

Frank's brows rose. "I guess the first step is to find out where Hammond Helbert really is. Somewhere there's a black suit with him in it."

Terry looked at the black suits. "The kids are running now," he said, his voice locked in the mystery of it all. "Where, I wonder."

Tim and Kelly ran along the inside of the wheel—the great inner tube. Their destination was the exercise room then, after whatever they were to do there, to the equipment room.

After a long silence, Tim said, "I wonder what's happening to Uncle Morty? Maybe he's behind us in the swamp right now."

"He could show up here any minute."

"Or not."

A man's voice sounded—a calm, electronic voice, prerecorded to give calm, thorough instructions. "Orbital sensors indicate approaching meteor. Auto-evasion not yet installed. Please report to the bridge to take evasive action."

"Bridge?" Tim repeated. "That's the structure in the middle of the large axle? A meteor? Maybe it's just a drill."

"Why would they have a drill when they could have the real thing in here? And that voice sounded like it wasn't kidding."

"We need to get to the axle."

At that instant a series of large red arrows appeared and began flashing, "Bridge." They pointed in the direction Tim and Kelly were already going.

The voice returned, "Indicators are that the meteor is traveling at an unusually high rate of speed. Suggest that all trainees hurry."

# CHAPTER 10

Tim and Kelly wasted no time responding to the warning about the meteor. They ran, leaped, and scrambled as fast as they could, following the arrows that flashed on the wall. They now pointed toward a round hole in the ceiling—another tube that went straight up.

"One of the wheel spokes," Tim suggested.

As if born to it, Tim and Kelly took their positions below the hole and leaped upward. The weightless world allowed them to fly side by side to the next level where the arrows pointed to another, larger tube perpendicular to the spoke—the axle.

Sirens began sounding, and the red arrows pulsed more rapidly. If the purpose was to force the kids to pump more adrenalin and move faster, it succeeded. They ran for all they were worth, their strides long and determined. After what seemed like forever, they came to a closed door. Opening it, they found another tube, this one heading straight up again. They leaped as they had before and came to a landing and another door. They threw that one open and were immediately confronted by a console of dials, meters, indicators, lights, and gauges just below a vast, panoramic view of the space station and the universe beyond.

Momentarily stunned, the kids hesitated for several heartbeats before the voice woke them. "You'd better do something," it said. "I'll highlight the meteor for you. Look at your screen."

The panoramic view must have been a huge telemonitoring screen, for instantly a foot-square window was drawn just below the sterile glow of the moon. At the center of the window was a speck—one that grew larger as they watched—heading right for them.

"Now call upon your training in Houston to guide the station away from trouble."

"I'm not sure I like this," Kelly said.

"You didn't go to Houston without me, did you?" Tim said.

"Not likely," Kelly replied, the concern in her voice approaching panic. "You're the one who's good with the tractor. What do we do? That thing's coming fast."

Tim didn't reply; instead he frantically searched the console for something that might help him do what the voice thought he already knew how to do. Anxiously he glanced up at the approaching meteor. Kelly was right. It was larger and blazing right for them.

Tim returned to the console. "This is like no tractor I've ever seen." But when he scanned the controls a second time, he noticed a square area that seemed more brilliantly lighted than the rest. There was a single word, "Thrusters," with twelve buttons below it—two each were labeled "right," "left," "up," "down," "forward," "back."

"This huge thing can't possibly be controlled by twelve buttons," Tim muttered.

"What did you find?"

"Let's find out."

Tim pressed the "up" buttons. On the screen he saw distant rockets ignite on the center connectors—one set on each end near each wheel. The space station groaned and creaked all around them and began to move quite slowly upward.

The voice came again, "Meteor trajectory now dead center."

Tim continued to press the "up" buttons. The space station continued to groan, and the thruster jets continued to fire—the station rose with deliberate slowness. But one of the jets must have produced more thrust than the other, for one end of the station rose faster than the other—the station began to turn.

"Meteor trajectory slightly lower than center." The voice remained calm, even if the words weren't. "It is closing fast. The station is beginning to yaw."

"What happens when a meteor hits a space station?" Kelly asked, staring at the growing meteor.

Tim didn't reply. He let up on the faster thruster and let the other catch up, then he reignited it. The station rose.

The voice came back. "Calculations indicate there will be an impact in three minutes. Impact point will be the bridge."

Four ears perked with shock, four eyes locked together.

"The bridge?" they cried together.

"Why didn't it tell us?" Kelly asked frantically.

"No time to complain. We've got to get out of here."

They both charged the door. Throwing it open they came to the vertical tube. Where before they had leaped up, now they had to dive down.

"Come on, there's no time to think about this now," Tim cried, trying desperately not to think about it. He grabbed his sister by the hand, and they dove into the tube headfirst.

Jumping up had been easy. There had been a Superman feeling about it. They had propelled themselves with their legs, reached above them with their arms, and moved with swift grace to the next level. But diving into a tube, into air, and hardly going anywhere at all was frightening. What made it even more frightening was the fact that at any second the world above them might explode and throw them into space—where there was no air, nothing to keep them alive. Their heads kept saying it was all "virtual"—but their hearts could already feel that future explosion and the air rushing away from them.

They couldn't get down the tube. They grabbed at its walls and walked their hands down it. But their progress was incredibly slow. Three minutes had to have ticked away by now. Yet they hadn't. Tim and Kelly grabbed at the wall again and again.

Suddenly they were at the axle door. It was locked. Maybe the station was already trying to isolate the point of impact. For whatever reason, the door wouldn't budge. Even after Tim banged on it, kicked it, tried the handle again and again, it remained locked.

The voice again, "Thirty seconds to impact."

Frantic, Kelly joined her brother's efforts. While trying to position herself beside him, she pushed against a panel just above the door. It gave way.

"It's loose!" Kelly cried. "Come on."

It opened like a door. Kelly dove through it, Tim following right behind her. The instant he was through, Kelly slammed the door shut. She heard it latch.

Where were they? Neither knew. They thought they were entering the axle they had come down, but this wasn't it.

"It must be the other side of the axle," Tim ventured. "The one attached to the other wheel."

This side was committed to agriculture. As far as they could see were crops of all kinds. Some they were familiar with—corn, soybean, wheat, even trees and flowers—some they weren't. Arcing above it was a glass roof. It was through this roof that the kids watched the approaching meteor. It was just a streak, a blurred bullet blazing through space—then it hit.

First it slammed into one of the cross tubes connecting the wheels, and the tube exploded. Steel girders were ripped and twisted like spaghetti, panels that defined the tube's walls shattered and were thrown off into space, tongues of flames erupted but were quickly extinguished, blackening the tube's new ragged edges. A few of the exploding panels spun like power saw blades cutting into an adjacent tube. It, too, burst. Though without the force of the first one, the pressurized inside blew out the panels near the cut, then exploded as electricity and chemicals and gases merged. Frantic sirens went off as if they were needed to warn Tim and Kelly of the danger.

They only saw the second series of explosions peripherally. Their eyes were riveted on the meteor as it continued on and blasted through the bridge tower. It entered one side of the sphere, blew out the other, and an instant later, the bridge detonated. A huge ball of flames engulfed the sphere. The space station superstructure buckled, the steel bones that held its body together bent like straw and the skin ripped like tin foil; debris blew out in all directions.

Another cross tube was struck. As before, after the cross tube's skin was violated, there was a blast, and the tube was torn completely in half. Again flames lapped at space then died. The meteor went through another connector tube. Great portions immediately disintegrated. Molten metal spewed out, following the meteor, then larger pieces broke loose—jagged edges, swirling and twisting against the black. Finally whole panels tore free—white squares also twisting and flying off. Another connecting tube was hit by debris and was severed completely.

As the meteor wreaked havoc upon *Freedom IV,* it plunged toward earth with debris in its wake.

The space station appeared crippled and vulnerable. It looked as if any second huge pieces of it would tear free and drift away, eventually to burn in earth's atmosphere. Or perhaps the entire space station—what remained of it—would do the same. Although some of the debris had come close, the axle Tim and Kelly were in was still intact.

"I think it took out the other side of the axle," Tim said, his voice trembling. "It was heading in that direction anyway."

Kelly said nothing. She stood near the glass and looked out. Now and then she saw a sputtering of flame or an electronic discharge or a weakened area of the station's skin erupting, throwing a panel off somewhere. Everything looked tenuous— like they were truly living on top of a pile of sand whose base was slipping swiftly away. "Why do I suddenly wish I were back on the farm?" she asked.

"I wish they'd turn those sirens off," Tim grumbled.

Only now did Kelly hear them again—irritating, urgent, frightening.

A female voice came—again calm, terribly calm—the calm only electronics can possess. "Damage assessment. Bridge is eliminated. Auxiliary environmental controls in place. Only connector tubes A32 and A44 currently able to support life. Necessary hatches closed to preserve atmosphere. Skin puncture analysis proceeding."

Another female voice—this one urgent. Now even the electronics were getting concerned. "Orbit degrading. Orbit degrading," it said.

"What's 'orbit degrading' mean?" Kelly called over the sirens.

They both got an answer immediately. Through the transparent roof of the tube, they saw the scene before them begin to change. The large, flat glow of the moon began slipping from view, the stars began swirling like they were part of a celestial kaleidoscope, the earth became more visible and slightly larger.

"Orbit degrading dramatically—urgent. Orbit degrading dramatically," an even more frightening tone in the electronic voice.

An instructor's voice came. "We know you don't want to hear this," it said. "But the station will reenter earth's atmosphere in twenty-three minutes, eighteen seconds—seventeen seconds—sixteen. You must evacuate. A shuttle is coming from *Freedom II*.

Retrieve your space suits and return to the air lock. They will pick you up shortly. Again, reentry in twenty-three minutes, nine seconds—eight seconds. You must be aboard the shuttle by then, or you will suffer the ultimate hot foot."

Tim groaned. "I hate humorous programmers."

Tim eyed his virtual watch. It showed 5:04. When it said 5:27 it would be too late.

Suddenly the tube they were in shuddered as if the strain of holding the station together was too much for it. There was the muffled cry of metal twisting, fighting the bolts and welds that restrained it. "The suits are in the air lock and the air lock's in the east wheel. We have to get to the other wheel by one of those two good tubes—which were they?" Tim spoke quickly.

"A-something—A32 and A44," Kelly replied, her eyes darting around looking for telltale signs that the station was tearing itself apart. Dying in a plane crash seemed like nothing compared to this.

"We'd better get going," Tim said. When Kelly didn't respond right away, he grabbed her hand and pulled her along. After about two steps, though, she came to life, said a quick prayer, and fell in beside her brother.

"How are we going to find A32 and A44?" Kelly asked as they ran beside a tall stand of corn.

"Let's hope for a map or something," Tim replied. "Maybe we'll stumble onto it."

That statement troubled Kelly for a minute, but only for a minute. There was no time to be troubled by anything. They had to get to the west wheel and find their way back to the east wheel before the station either broke up or burned up in the earth's atmosphere. Neither prospect suited her. But more important, they had to get out of "NASA-land" as fast as possible and find the VR control room.

Tim knew their priorities too. He ran, leaped, and even flew a couple of times beside the massive varieties of plants and trees toward what he hoped was an exit. "This is going to take forever," he finally complained, the end of the tunnel still not in sight.

"You'd think they'd have a people-mover or something—a space Amtrak."

The moment the words were out of Kelly's mouth they came to a golf cart-sized car on tracks, the tracks reaching off toward the distant exit. Without a word they jumped aboard. Kelly quickly studied the control panel. It wasn't a difficult choice—forward, backward, stop. She hit the button marked "forward." The car came alive. Its whirring electronic sound merged with the frantic sirens, and within seconds they were zipping ahead past narrow fields of beans, tomatoes, grapes, and other crops, as well as small groves of trees and shrubs. The kids relaxed for a moment.

"I thought they'd been eating a bunch of pills and things instead of growing their own food," Tim mused, sitting back in the plastic seat. "If the track doesn't end—or something worse—we should be all right."

Kelly leaned back and allowed her heart to slow a little. Finally she said, "Do you think it was Jesus who led us to that open panel? Or someone else?"

"Above the door back there, you mean?"

"We would have never known it was there," she said, still a little mystified by their good fortune.

"Even if it was someone else, I guess it was ultimately the Lord. Dad says he uses people."

"So someone might be taking care of us in here," she said, the statement a curious realization.

"You think it was *someone* and not just *something* that happened?" Tim asked. "We are talking VR here—strange things happen."

"They seem to be happening often. We got separated from Uncle Morty—we're still free; he may not be. The tree fell and distracted the snakes. The water froze—and then unfroze on our enemy. Lightning hit the tree so I could get over the canyon, and the panel opened to this garden axle. And there's the maps with the flashing control room. Trainees wouldn't care about the control room. I'm beginning to think something extraordinary is going on."

"What about the glow of the instrument panel on the bridge?" Tim added, catching Kelly's train of thought. "It would have taken me forever to find those controls."

Suddenly they heard more cries of metal straining, a high-pitched yowl as joints and seams tore apart what little remained of the space station.

The sound unnerved Kelly, sending her eyes darting around. Tim froze, eyes fixed above, staring out the transparent roof at the twisted damage until the sounds subsided.

"I don't like this," Kelly said, her eyes finally coming to rest on her brother.

"We're helpless. Just waiting for this tube to twist apart and pop—like one of those Pillsbury dough things."

"I'll never look at biscuits the same way again."

"Look—the exit!" Tim exclaimed.

Appearing out of the distant mist was the broad, arching door leading to the west wheel. The wheel itself loomed large outside. Seconds later the car stopped before the door and they leaped out. Bursting through it they entered the wheel's hub, a series of spokeholes radiating from it.

"Which one of these holes do we jump through?" Kelly asked.

"Maybe there's a map," Tim said, turning right and left looking for one.

Nothing.

Without a word, Kelly threw open the door to the axle again and ran inside. Through the glass ceiling she studied each of the cross tubes. "There," she cried, pointing to the side. "That one's A32—it's written on the side." It was also the only one on that side of the space station that remained untouched by the explosions. Tubes above and below it had been ruptured near their midpoints.

"This spoke should get us near there," Tim told her when she returned.

As if in warning, the space station groaned again. The earth's gravitational pull must be increasing and with it the wounded station's instability.

"We'd better get going," Tim said and launched himself into the spoke. But he only went a few feet into it. It was closed off by a tight metal hatch. He spun around and left the spoke just as Kelly was about the follow him in. "It's closed off," he said. He grabbed the handle to the axle door and threw it open. Looking toward the other side of the space station he quickly found A44, the other functioning tube. Just as he was about to return to the wheel's hub he saw an explosion out of the corner of his eye. One of the already damaged tubes near A32 erupted. A tongue of fire belched from the side, sending several molten skin plates spinning into space. One of them, spinning like a saw blade, struck tube A32 and tore a gaping hole in it.

A female voice said, "Cross tube A-32 out of service."

Heaving a relieved sigh, Tim returned to the hub. Kelly looked concerned as he returned. "What happened?"

"A32 got clobbered."

"Could the same thing happen to A44?"

"Probably best not to think about it. Come on, this should be the spoke to take us to it." Without hesitation, because he knew hesitation would only scare him further, Tim leaped into the spoke. After a huge breath for courage, Kelly followed.

The main lights must have given out, for now there were only thin light strips traveling the length of the tube beside them.

Again the station groaned, this time a sorrowful, mind-numbing squall. Although muffled, they heard the tearing of metal.

"I hope that's not A44," Tim called back to Kelly.

"I hope it's not this spoke."

It wasn't. After a few moments they emerged from it to the wheel. It felt strange sweeping down from the ceiling and gently landing on the floor.

"There's A44," Tim called the instant his feet hit the floor.

After a short run, they came to the entrance of the long tube and found another small cart on tracks waiting for them. When they were seated, Tim stabbed the "forward" button and the car took off. It zipped along past offices and conference rooms— all empty and expectant—past windows where they caught frequent glimpses of the extensive damage the meteor and the resulting explosions had caused.

"Look at the axle," Kelly exclaimed.

The meteor had passed through the bridge and slashed through the east side of the axle, the side they had traveled to get to the bridge. That side of the axle now hung loose, its ravaged edge charred, sparks still erupting there.

"I think that would fall under the category of close call," Tim mused.

"I'm surprised the station's holding together at all," Kelly said darkly.

"Maybe it's not," Tim replied, his eyes now glued to a spot on the tube's interior maybe fifty yards ahead. It looked like a tear—but it couldn't be. All the air would have leaked out. Whatever it was, though, he was sure it wasn't good.

Another frightening chorus of high-pitched yowls erupted from the straining metals. Instantly Tim determined what that something was: a wrinkle in the tube's skin, a twist, like a rag when wrung. As they approached the wrinkle, Tim saw more of them radiating from the larger one. There had to be significant strain on the tube at that point—maybe they were about the midpoint between the wheels. They passed below it and went about twenty yards when there was another cry of twisting metal, this one close, deafening, and unlike the others. It ended in a frightening pop.

Tim turned around toward the direction of the sound. "Oh, no!" he gasped. The twist they had just passed below was now a yawning tear. Black space sprawled beyond it, and their precious air began escaping through it.

# CHAPTER 11

Frank Holloway climbed into a waiting unmarked black Ford Taurus and was driven to the FBI building. Going to the third floor he was met by Special Agent Mike Dunhill. Frank and Mike had never worked together before, but when Frank had called his usual FBI contact and described the situation, Mike's name was mentioned. A friend of Uncle Morty, Mike had been the special agent assigned to the Crafts' last encounter with Virtual Reality.

Dunhill joined Frank in the third floor computer room, a secure area bathed in artificial light with the smell of purified air. Mike Dunhill wore a deep blue suit, white shirt, and maroon striped tie. With his black hair and penetrating eyes, he was the picture of what an FBI special agent was supposed to look like.

"Hammond Helbert," Mike repeated the name. "I knew he'd come back sooner or later. I guess it's sooner."

"Who is he?"

"The brother of the inventor of the Virtual Reality computer. He's bad news. He's also very hard to find."

"You've tried."

"And are continuing to."

"You've probably done all the usual things—go through tax records for an address, check utility companies, financial institutions."

"All of it. PO boxes in different parts of the country. Doesn't seem to care about his mail, anyway. What's he done now?"

"We just need to find him," Frank said, refusing to say more.

"Does it have to do with that computer?"

"I guess I can tell you that."

"He's in Virtual Reality?"

"Seems to be."

"But no black suit in sight?"

"Not his, anyway."

"Any cabling to a telecommunications unit?"

"Let's say no."

Mike thought for a moment. "He's coming in through micro-wave—high speed, very high speed."

"Can you monitor that stuff?"

"If it exists we can monitor it. Maybe we can trace it. It's not like tracing a phone call, but if we can nail down the addressing schemes there might be something we can do."

Now it was Frank's turn to think. The more people who knew about the president being locked in the black suit the more opportunity for the story to get out. Even the FBI might get careless when dealing with a story this important.

Finally he said, "I may be back."

"It's so big you don't want to work with us?" said Mike.

"We just don't want you guys getting all the credit."

Mike laughed softly, not sure whether to believe him or not.

◎

"What happened?" Kelly cried.

"The tube's—" But Tim didn't finish his sentence. Suddenly a white metal divider shot up from the floor, sealing the tube from the effects of the tear behind them.

"It's okay again," Kelly said with great relief.

The car hurled forward while both wondered how long it would remain okay.

It wasn't long. Another cry of metal, this one like the last—more than metal straining, again the telltale sound of ripping. This time the car shuddered and dropped slightly. They eyed the track ahead. It seemed solid. But they heard that rushing sound again. The kids spun in their seats. Above the now distant metal divider, the tube's roof tore again, the rip pushing several feet beyond the divider.

Another metal divider rose from the floor and sealed the tube off. Air rushed in to replace the air that had escaped.

More tearing metal. The roof above the new divider ripped open. The roar of escaping air. Another divider appeared and sealed the tube off. The car shuddered.

This time the instant the new divider was in place the tear in the roof extended beyond it. This time the next divider was only a few yards from the rear of their speeding car.

"The tube's twisting and tearing," Tim cried. In the distance the exit sign appeared. "A couple more minutes and we're there," he shouted, renewed hope buoying him.

Suddenly the tearing sound became a deep, aching scream. It cried out from not only the tube's skin but now from its superstructure. Iron beams buckled about thirty yards ahead. Fortunately the skin remained air tight. Unfortunately, the cart carrying them jumped its track, the tracks having buckled as well. Tim and Kelly were catapulted from the car like cannon-balls. Flying and spinning uncontrollably, Kelly slapped against the wall, while Tim ricocheted off the ceiling and slammed against a nearby planter, his side bending around it like a pretzel.

But there was no time to be slowed by pain. A massive, jagged tear had breached the divider just behind the cart. Instantly air was being sucked into space, producing an incredible updraft. Kelly sensed herself being lifted from the floor toward the midnight of space beyond the tear. At first it was just a feeling, but then the pressure grabbed her and yanked her toward the tear and the space beyond.

Kelly screamed. Tim had just started fighting the sucking pressure himself when he saw Kelly in trouble. Like the eye of a tornado, she was being swept up in the escaping air. A decorative tree was planted nearby. Tim grabbed a limb in one hand and reached out and latched onto Kelly's ankle with the other. For a moment he thought he was going to lose her, but he didn't. His grip held.

"We've got to get out of here," Tim cried. "It'll seal us in here any minute!" Worse, though, air was getting scarce, and it was becoming more difficult to breathe.

Kelly didn't hear him. The cyclone roar of air was too loud. Worse yet, she thought she felt Tim's grip begin to give way. "Hold on—please. I'm gone if you don't."

Suddenly a divider shot up from the floor missing Kelly by only inches. The instant it was sealed, the pull on her ceased as replacement air rushed in. Tim's firm grip pulled her down beside him.

Tim's eyes anxious, his lungs gasping the new air, he managed a single word, "Run!"

Kelly didn't wait for another. Legs scrambling, she ran with all she had. Tim scrambled too, but he could not overtake his sister. When the exit was only twenty yards away, the tear breached the newest divider. Like a dagger thrusting at them, it roared along the ceiling then twisted down the wall as iron support beams twisted and bent. The tube seemed about to break off from the wheel. If that happened they'd be thrown off into space.

Air escaped, this time with hurricane force as it was pulled from the wheel as well. Tim and Kelly were instantly caught up in the suction. At first they kept from being overcome by clinging to anything lashed down—furniture, doorways—and using them like rungs of a ladder.

Suddenly the rip overtook them, and the draft was nearly more than they could manage. The beams twisted and cried mournfully.

The exit was only a few feet away.

But for Kelly it might as well have been a football field away. Her strength had all but given out, her grip on the arm of a chair was slipping. Seeing that she had slowed to a stop, Tim grabbed her arm.

"Only a little more—that hatch will close soon—we have to make it," he encouraged.

Kelly nearly cried that it was no use. But she couldn't give up. She had no idea how the suit would simulate floating through an airless space. Was she now literally facing her first real life-or-death situation? After a quick prayer she called up all her remaining energy. It wasn't much, but with a quick pull of her arms, she dove into the wheel's circular corridor.

To her joy, Tim flew in right behind her. The instant they cleared the hatch and were safely within the wheel, the tube hatch shut behind them.

They were safe. For now.

Tim eyed his virtual watch. 5:17. Ten minutes until the shuttle arrived.

In the distance they saw the menagerie sign glowing. The air lock and their space suits were just beyond it. "I think we've made it," he said breathlessly.

A man's voice patched in on the station's broadcast system sounded over the pulsing sirens. "This is *Shuttle Eagle II*. We'll be docking in ten minutes, maybe less. We can't afford to wait around so be there when we are. The station's breaking up and taking a nosedive faster than originally calculated."

Uncle Morty's excitement from having communicated to the president's staff outside had long since evaporated. The president's reaction had helped dampen his mood.

"They already knew I was a prisoner in here. They had to know. I didn't surround myself with stupid people. Nothing's changed. I'm still in here with no way out."

Since then, the father and son had fallen into an uneasy silence. Gar sat on the prairie floor leaning against a rigid buffalo leg while the big mouse sat in the corner where two invisible walls joined. Neither looked at the other.

Morty prayed.

For a genius, helplessness was an unusual feeling. Morty had always been able to draw together small, sometimes seemingly unrelated pieces of information to form creative and useful ideas. But not this time. Since computers did only what they were programmed to do, they were absolutely inflexible sometimes. This computer had them in a tightly constructed box and had no intention of letting them out.

Frustration gave way to despair, another unusual feeling for Uncle Morty. The Lord was still in charge, he knew. The Lord's promise that all things would work out to his good was still in force. Yet there was a strong part of Uncle Morty that relied on himself and his own mental power, and when those resources proved to be of no value, he became discouraged.

*No,* he said to himself. *There's a reason we're here.* A question formed on his lips. "Mr. President?"

The mouse looked up.

"Do you love your son?" Morty asked him.

The president's eyes widened, and he cleared his throat as if fumbling with his emotions. "Of course I love my son," he replied. But he didn't look at Gar.

"Do you realize that any minute now he might be put through some excruciating pain?"

"We all might," the president responded.

"Do you know how VR works concerning pain?" Morty pressed.

"Why don't you tell me?" the president said with a note of sarcasm.

"Sewn into the fabric of the VR suit are thousands of sensation producers—little microchips at the junctions of wires. When two wires are activated, the sensation triggered by the voltage is released. VR was pretty primitive when I talked last with Matthew Helbert, the developer. But it doesn't have to simulate pain—it's real. Pain is pain, and it is produced by varying degrees of electric shock. The original idea was to give a quick, painful shock as a warning. Nothing prolonged, not too severe. I understand, though, that the three former owners have intensified the 'simulation.' Pain now can be severe and prolonged."

Morty looked up at the frozen wall of buffalo. "Imagine how it would feel for that herd to trample you. My feeling is that Hammond Helbert has chosen something that will produce the maximum effect—turn the voltage up as high as it will go and keep it there for as long as he can. Your son may experience something he will never forget—it might even kill him. And if you weren't president, he wouldn't be here."

"If I weren't president he wouldn't be living in the White House or able to afford toys like this. He wouldn't be written up in magazine articles or be sought by the top colleges—no matter what his grades are." The mouse got to his feet now and began pacing. "Kids today think the world revolves around them. It doesn't. We parents make things happen for them. And what appreciation do we get? We get locked up in a black suit. I might as well be in a rubber room bouncing off the walls."

"But how can you talk to someone you love like that?"

"Love is meaningless," the president said in a voice brittle with ice. "You tell me what it is. No, I'll tell you what it is. It's doing for the other person, that's what it is. And I do everything for him." A rigid finger went up and stabbed at the air in Gar's direction. "I give him a place to live—a warm, safe place. He wants for nothing—food, clothing, computers! He comes and goes as he likes, within reason. He's got it made. I love my son, and don't you ever think I don't."

"I'm sure you do," Morty said, his voice softer.

"I've got responsibilities—responsibilities he and you don't understand. I have to fulfill them, work hard on them, be there when I'm needed." The president leaned against a transparent wall again. "Love is a bunch of sentimental hogwash."

Morty gave up. He was a computer jockey, not a psychologist or philosopher. He did know two things though. In a twisted way, the president was right. Love, as the Lord defines it in the Bible, is doing for others. The good Samaritan sacrificed for the injured man; Jesus went to the cross for his people. But Morty knew something else too. There was more to love than that—there was kindness and respect and commitment and forgiveness—cheerful forgiveness.

Morty could bring none of that about. Not between these two anyway. Not right now.

Despair returned, and he again began to fight it off.

He once more scanned their little prison. On one side the buffalo were poised to barrel right over them. On the other three sides were transparent walls—like glass. Nothing had changed. The three of them were still stuck.

He prayed again. But when the prayer was done, nothing had changed.

What were Tim and Kelly doing? Were they okay? Or were they facing some other menace? He still received no answer.

回

Kelly lay on the east wheel's floor on her back, her arms stretched out. She breathed heavily, filling herself with the revitalizing oxygen. Finally she asked her brother, "You okay?"

Tim groaned and grabbed a couple of lungfuls of air. "We should make it all right," he said. "The air lock is just beyond the cages."

"I'd forgotten about the monkeys," Kelly said, struggling to a sitting position. "Maybe we should try to take them with us."

Tim sat up. "Monkeys?" He stood as did Kelly. "They're virtual monkeys."

"It's like Harve. You wouldn't let Harve die would you?"

"They're not like Harve. They're monkeys."

"You wouldn't let Sonya die?"

That stopped him. "Sonya—that's different from a monkey."

He felt his heart stir at the thought of the beautiful girl he had met in their last VR adventure. He longed to meet her again.

"They're all virtual. All the same. Come on. It'll only take a minute. The key's hanging right there beside them."

But as they approached the cages, to their surprise, they didn't hear any chirps or grunts. They also saw no movement. Concerned, they moved even faster. When they finally stood before the cages, their hearts leaped to their throats.

The gibbon cage was empty, its bars pried apart to make a hole large enough for a man to walk through. The bars on the other cages were also pried apart. But the spider monkey and the orangutan hadn't escaped. They lay on the bottom of their cages—dead, their bodies contorted as if beaten and twisted. The sight sent a shiver of fear crawling up Tim's and Kelly's spines.

"Something's loose," Kelly gasped. "Something violent. I hate violence."

"And if it is big enough to kill the ape . . ."

"It's big enough to do us some damage," Kelly finished Tim's terrifying thought and immediately spun around, her eyes scanning everything. Nothing looked out of the ordinary.

"The air lock is not far. Let's just get out of here and onto that shuttle. We've only got seven minutes, anyway," Tim said.

There was no need for Kelly to respond. With frequent glances over their shoulders, they ran as quickly as they could to the air lock door.

They got there with five minutes to spare.

Tim could feel himself relax. It would be a pleasure to end an adventure without some kind of dramatic chase or death-defying maneuver—crawling on his belly blindly over an alligator-infested canyon for example. All they had to do now was get into their space suits and climb aboard the shuttle. He could hardly wait.

Kelly, too, sensed that the heartrending excitement was at an end, at least for now, and that the shuttle would, somehow, take them out of NASA-land so they could begin looking for the control room.

Tim stabbed the door button and the door lifted. He stepped casually inside the air lock, but Kelly hesitated. Something didn't look right, but she couldn't put her finger on what it was. The air lock door wasn't that crisp, reflective metal it once was. Now it looked fuzzy and black. When it began to unroll itself—huge arms appeared and then a massive face—a gibbon's face with a round jaw and those black liquid eyes. It hissed where the lips parted to reveal sharp, yellow teeth—large teeth, easily able to rip Tim and Kelly in half.

Kelly gasped, grabbed Tim by the arm, and spun him around.

It still took him a second to realize what was staring him in the face. But when he did, he yelped and dove from the room, his weightlessness propelling him against the far wall. Kelly followed, and the instant she was clear she punched the air lock door button and closed the huge monkey inside.

They realized there was both good and bad in this. Now the door protected them from Supermonkey in there, but he also stood between them and escape.

"He's huge," Kelly gasped. "How'd he get so big?"

"We have four minutes," Tim groaned. "How are we going to get him out of there in four minutes?"

"You don't happen to have a thirty-foot banana with you? Maybe a one-ton peanut?"

"I could coax him out," Tim suggested breathlessly. "If he chases me, you could get away. After all, you let me go first across the canyon. Now it's your turn."

Kelly got to her feet. "Where's the space door controls in there?"

Tim thought. "There's one by the space door. There might be one by this door, too, but I'm not sure. You know we're down to three minutes."

A voice from the rescue shuttle was patched through. "We've docked just outside the air lock. We'll be waiting for you. We have a new calculation. You have two minutes—maybe less."

"Less!" Tim exploded. "We've got the Mighty Kong to deal with."

"Okay, Lord, what now?" Kelly muttered to herself. An instant later a thought struck. "Give me your belt," she cried.

The blue jumpsuits they wore had cloth belts. When Kelly had both of them, she joined them together at the buckle. She quickly told her brother her plan.

"You sure?" Tim asked as if he thought her insane.

"It'll work," she assured him, though she had no idea whether it would.

Realizing there was no time to argue, Tim crouched by the side of the air lock door. Gripping his end of the belt, he watched while Kelly wrapped her end tightly around her hand.

"Ready?" she asked.

"Sure," Tim said without conviction.

Kelly heaved a deep breath for courage, punched the air lock door button, and stood before it. The door rose with a *whoosh!* The monster monkey's mug had probably been pressed against it and was now inches from Kelly's nose.

Kelly screamed.

The monkey spread its lips across yellow teeth and hissed.

Kelly back-stepped, then turned and dove. The monkey cried a terrifying sound and lunged.

Its powerful legs propelled it forward. Had Kelly been there, it would have slammed into her and carried her to the opposite wall. But she wasn't. Holding on to the belt, Tim swung her around carrying her back in a wide arc to the wall next to Tim. Without hesitation, while the monkey struggled to regain itself, Tim and Kelly spun around the corner into the air lock. Tim punched the button that brought the door down.

"It worked!" Tim exhaled. "Let's get our space suits on and get out of here."

Tim's virtual watch read exactly 5:26 as he and Kelly climbed into the shuttle through the open, fifteen-foot cargo bay on top—not a moment to spare. The bay doors closed above them as they moved into the passenger compartment. To their surprise, they found Barney sitting at the shuttle controls—a cockpit below four windows that included two rotational hand controllers, three TV screens, air speed and altitude indicators, a radio panel, and other gauges and indicators. Barney wore the same blue and red uniform they wore beneath their space suits.

"Well, now, Gov'nor," Barney greeted, his familiar English accent a song to their ears.

"Barney!" Tim greeted. There was little headroom in the shuttle, so Tim had to bend over in order to keep from hitting his head as he wriggled out of his space suit. "Good to see you. Very good."

"Good to 'ave you back."

Kelly wriggled out of her suit more easily. They hung them on the hooks provided. She was about to speak when she noticed, as did Tim, that the space station, now twisted and void of its former glory, gained speed, diving toward the fuzzy envelope that cocooned the earth.

A moment later sparks erupted at its forward points; the skin burned away, quickly exposing what superstructure was left. Then the superstructure began to melt, the sparks devouring the station as it plunged toward earth. A minute or two later the station was only a glowing memory, a shooting star. Then it was extinguished.

"That could have been us burning up down there," Tim mused gravely. "Now it's just a big virtual monkey."

"I wonder what VR does if the thing you're a part of dies. What would have happened to us?"

"I don't want to find out."

"Well," said Barney in a cheerful tone. "I think it's time to take you back to Earth for further training."

"We hope to get out of NASA altogether," Tim said.

"Whatever," Barney replied, beginning to work the controls.

"Hey, Barney," Kelly asked, "do you know how to get to the VR control room?"

Barney eyes became thoughtful. "Yes."

"How?"

"Can't say. Not here. Not now."

"When? Where?"

"On the outside."

"Outside of VR?"

"Outside of here."

"Is that where we're going now?"

"Don't know. But you will soon. Very soon."

Kelly nodded. Computer characters only know what they know at the time they know it. No more. It would be useless to question him further. She sat in the seat next to Tim. After buckling herself in, she asked, "What do you think?"

"About what?"

"About the monkey."

"The big banana idea definitely might have worked," Tim said.

"There was something different about it."

"It was big."

"But it started out small and was *made* big."

"And?"

"Until now we've always had something or someone working *for* us. Anything bad that happened was just Virtual Reality being itself. But this time someone *made* something bad happen to us."

Tim's eyes widened as Kelly's words sank in. Before, they seemed to have a powerful friend. Now it looked like they had a powerful enemy too.

The thought sent a brittle chill into his heart. The last thing they needed was an enemy in here.

# CHAPTER 12

Leaning back in his virtual chair in the virtual saloon, Hammond Helbert grunted disappointedly. Those lousy kids had gotten off the space station in spite of the meteor and the monkey. But, he told himself, those were only experiments—and they'd been successful—in a way. Now he knew he could truly make their lives miserable, and that knowledge was important.

He longed for a drink—water—anything. He knew he couldn't get a drink in VR. There was no such thing as a virtual drink or a virtual burger.

He wanted this whole thing over so he could relax somewhere.

But it would only be over when those stupid kids got what was coming to them, either alone or with their uncle when he got his. Only then could he relax again.

Where would they go next? Assuming Matthew was pulling strings for them, he wouldn't let them come to Hammond's western village.

Hammond punched in a command, and a map appeared on the little screen. He punched in another command, and after a second or two the computer displayed more information. Tim and Kelly's trek was represented by a dashed line on the map. It ran through the swamp, then meandered through the space station and into the shuttle. Alongside the space station was the CIA training area. Strangely enough, Hammond had the most success working with the programmer there. When the CIA took delivery of the VR machine, Hammond figured he would never be able to break their security. As it turned out, the programmer was so worried about his job that he actually encouraged Hammond's involvement.

"So," Hammond said to himself, "it's time not only to get my revenge, but to beat that brother of mine."

"It's getting hot in here," Kelly said. A bead of sweat rolled down her cheek.

They were still sitting in the passenger seats aboard the shuttle. Tim didn't respond, but he, too, brushed perspiration from his cheek. "What's going on, Barney?" he asked.

Barney sat in the pilot's chair, his eyes glued to the controls. The shuttle pushed through the earth's atmosphere, nose high, its belly taking the heat of the approach. "We're at entry interface—reentry," Barney said, his English accent thick. "We just broke through 400,000 feet, sixty-five nautical miles."

"Is it always this hot?" Kelly asked, feeling quite uncomfortable.

Barney shook his head. "It gets 'ot out there—up to three thousand degrees Fahrenheit. But not in 'ere—not like this anyway. There might be something wrong. There's thousands of silica tiles out there taking the brunt of the heat."

"So why so hot in here?"

Barney went to work scanning controls, pushing this button and that. "We normally lose a few tiles—no more than a hundred. Looks like we've already lost more'n a thousand."

Kelly didn't like the sound of that at all. "Are we burning up?" she asked, getting to her feet and moving to the cockpit next to Barney.

"We've stabilized—doesn't look like we're losing any more." A moment later Barney announced, "TAEM 'as kicked in—Terminal Area Energy Management. We've hit 2,500 feet per second. It'll make sure we've got proper airspeed, altitude, and heading for landing. We're in good shape."

"Kelly, that thing'll fly the shuttle without your help," Tim called to her. "Come back here."

Reluctantly she returned to her seat.

In an effort to take her mind off their approach, Tim asked, "Where do you think we'll go next?"

"What's left? CIA-land? It sure would be nice to end up near the VR control room."

"Haven't so far."

Kelly had no desire to go through another training exercise, least of all something to do with the CIA—with spies and terrorists. She sighed deeply and said, "I think we're just going to burn up."

"We can't burn up," Tim said as if he knew. "None of the shuttles ever burn up. It's just hot."

Suddenly they heard an alarm. The rasping, high-pitched noise, much the sound they had just left on the space station, reverberated off the walls as if they were inside a bell.

"What's that?" Tim jumped.

Barney didn't answer right away. He peered at the bank of controls. Finally he straightened. "We're losing tiles again. Hmm—not good."

"Not good!?" Kelly shouted.

"That's what it's saying, 'Not good,'" Barney replied, pointing to a small display, the words flashing there—his head darting here and there, focusing on this meter and that gauge. The computer character was into his frantic role.

The heat became more intense, breaking more sweat loose. It rolled down Kelly's brow, down her cheeks, back, and chest—her clothing began to chafe uncomfortably. "How hot can this suit get?" she finally asked when she was beginning to feel faint.

"I don't know," Tim groaned. "Probably hotter."

"Bad news, a crack in the underbelly has developed," Barney said, his voice strained. "We *are* going to burn up."

"We're going to what?" Tim questioned, sure he hadn't heard that.

"Says here we're going to burn up." He pointed to the display. The message flashed—"You're going to burn up."

"Why would they display that?" Tim exclaimed.

"We can't!" Kelly argued. "How can we virtually burn up? Wow, this is miserable!" Kelly felt like she was standing in an oven, the stifling heat boiling up around her.

Tim's eyes burned as sweat flowed into them. He blinked and shook his head, trying to shake the beads away. With helmet and visor in the way, there was no way to rub his eyes to cleanse them. "I can hardly see they burn so bad."

Suddenly flames engulfed the windows—yellow, red, angry flames.

"How far can this go?" Tim cried.

"Well," said Barney, his face glowing with the flames' reflection, "there is an answer to that."

"What?" Tim asked, his eyes inflamed.

"The answer is that it goes this far—it's the programmer's way of saying hello." Barney laughed. "I'll see you guys later." He waved.

Suddenly the hot, flaming world around them dissolved to darkness.

"You mean that was a joke?" Kelly cried as the heat faded. "I suppose if they turned us into french fries they would have had a real laugh."

"It's over, that's all that matters." Cool air had never felt so welcome to Tim.

Kelly groaned. "He never told us where the control room was."

They were no longer in space. They stood at the crest of a grassy knoll in the luscious shade of a large, sprawling oak. Below them, maybe a hundred yards away, was a carnival. A riot of colored lights—reds, blues, whites, sparkling strings of them—outlined everything. Adding to the color were flashing signs scattered around: Ferris Wheel, Fun House, Loop-the-Loop, Merry-Go-'Round. They all combined to light the valley. Above it all floated a huge, red-, white-, and blue-starred balloon, its passenger gondola suspended and tied about fifteen feet off the ground. Cheerful sounds rose up from it all—calliope music and bubbling voices—kids with balloons, other kids running around calling to one another and screaming, parents ushering their families around, and teens hand in hand.

"Hey, if this is the CIA place," Tim said, a smile spreading across his face, "these CIA guys know how to have fun."

Kelly just shook her head for a moment and put hands on her hips. "We don't have time to have fun."

"But maybe fun will come along by accident."

Kelly just sighed.

"You're really not getting into the spirit of this thing. Finally we've come someplace that makes sense. Come on. Let's see what it's all about."

Kelly nodded but didn't move.

"What's wrong?" Tim asked.

Kelly sighed again. "I guess I'm tired. No. That's not it. What's Dad call it? Shell shock. In the past two hours we've been chased by big snakes and alligators, blown out of the sky, and nearly fried—as a joke I might add. I need to catch my breath."

"You said we didn't have time—seconds matter."

"I know I said that—but we don't know that really. We could be the ones who are lost. Uncle Morty, the president and his son could be sitting somewhere with Cokes, eating ranch style chips while we run around getting blown up and fried. I'm taking a five-minute rest. Believe me, at the end of that five minutes nothing will have changed. Nothing."

"What's all this?" Terry Baker asked as two men in cheap suits and grease under their fingernails entered the basement room of the White House. They pushed a dolly with several black, lockable cases on it. Terry was speaking to Frank Holloway, who followed them.

"Went to see the FBI. They've been looking for Mr. Helbert too."

"Did they have any idea where to start?"

"One. That's why these two gentlemen are here."

While Terry and Frank spoke, the two technicians set up their equipment. They opened the cases and took out a small display. After hooking up cables to a fan-sized dish, they set the dish down by the computer.

"What are they doing?"

"Monitoring microwaves," one of the technicians said, probably tired of being ignored.

"Are you going to cut them off?" Terry asked, a little alarmed.

"No," Frank whispered to him, "if they take Hammond Helbert out of Virtual Reality we'll never get the president out. Helbert's got to let him out. They're trying to find out where the signal is coming from."

The other technician, now freed up while his partner monitored the signal, said, "Microwaves travel line of sight, from dish to dish. The dish either forwards the signal or channels it to a local network. We'll probably have to trace the signal through several dishes—maybe a satellite."

"The transmission is very fast—maybe in the gigabyte range," the technician by the display said. "Too fast for the monitor."

"You're kidding," Frank said, exasperated.

"We never kid," said the technician.

Frank believed him.

"It's a strange setup. Usually there's an elaborate disk configuration. This seems to bypass that."

"Can you trace it?" Frank asked.

"Not the way we wanted to. But maybe we can give you some directional help."

"Give me what you can," Frank told him.

The man nodded and went back to work on the keyboard and display.

"Who have you notified?" Terry asked Frank.

"Nobody. These guys don't even know why they're here. And better not ever tell anyone *that* they were here."

"Never in a million years," the technician at the display reaffirmed without moving his eyes from the readout.

"What are they doing?" the other technician asked, pointing at the black suits.

"An experiment."

"I've got something," the technician at the display announced.

▣

Kelly didn't rest the full five minutes. She couldn't. Her curiosity got the better of her. The lights and cheerful music were too intriguing to ignore. After only a few minutes she got up, walked over to Tim, and grabbed his arm. "I know what you're hoping to find down there," she said, pulling him along.

"Do you think she'll be there?"

"I hope not—we have to get through there quickly."

But that didn't stop Tim from grinning with anticipation. Sonya had been forbidden fruit the last time—plus, she was a computer character, the figment of an animator's imagination. But she was beautiful. A little older than Tim, she had raven hair, deep almond eyes, and soft haunting features that had been hard to forget—of course, Tim hadn't tried that hard.

Even though Kelly was reminding him of their ultimate mission, she reveled in the spring air and the soft pink glow of sunset spreading across the horizon. It was a welcome relief from burning up in the space shuttle. Birds sang somewhere in the distance. There were many evenings like this back home—after many a picnic with her mother. Her mother loved picnics, and on a day like this she was apt to finish the minimum of work and usher Tim and Kelly down to the lake for one.

Kelly longed for a picnic. She was suddenly glad she hadn't gone behind her mother's back with Bernie. That kiss would have been nice, but she hated the idea of being dishonest.

But still, the kiss would been nice. Her mother was just being overprotective.

"Why would she be down there, anyway?" came her brother's voice.

"Who?"

"Sonya."

"Ah, relax brother, dear. She's just a cartoon—but you know that."

"My attraction to her does seem a little weird."

They had walked about halfway down the grassy path and were passing a small stand of trees when they heard a voice calling to them over the noise from below.

Tim stopped, turned, and saw a shadowy figure standing there.

"You want us?" Tim asked cautiously.

"Who else?"

Tim walked to the edge of the trees.

"Be careful," Kelly warned, remaining back.

"I need you both in here," the voice said in a forced whisper.

"We can hear you out here," Tim told him.

"So can everyone else. Get in here."

Tim glanced at Kelly, shrugged, then stepped into the shadows. Kelly hesitated, but followed. The guy was no more than a black silhouette. "Who are you?" Kelly asked.

"Doesn't matter," the shadow said. "We don't use names here. I saw you arrive. You're with the company, right?"

"Company? Like Amway or something?"

"The company," the man insisted.

"Sure—the company," Kelly said, not really caring if they were or weren't.

"Good. He's hidden it somewhere in the carnival down there. We're not sure where. Your job is to find it and get it back to us."

"He's hidden *what*—and who is *he*?" Tim asked.

The dark figure shook his head in frustration. "The trigger—for the hydrogen bomb. It's hidden somewhere in there. But you won't be looking for it alone. Two terrorist groups have followed him and also want the trigger."

"Two groups?" Kelly exclaimed. "Why did there have to be any?"

The shadow shook his head even more impatiently. "You're kidding, right? Haven't you been briefed? Who are you people?"

"We're from the company, but we haven't been briefed," Tim said quickly.

The man was clearly annoyed. "Okay—but I'm asking for a raise. Now, we don't have much time. A member of the Russian Mafia—organized crime—has stolen the triggering mechanism for a nuclear device. Two terrorist groups want it. The Russian has been chased to the carnival down there and has hidden it. Both groups want to either buy it or steal it. You have to find the trigger and get it back to me. Understand? If either of the terrorist groups gets it you'll be going through this again. Any questions?"

Kelly turned toward the fair. She liked fairs. Her folks took them every year to the Wisconsin State Fair. They would enter a few cows in the competition, their mother would enter her jams and jellies, and her dad just would talk to the other farmers to see how they were doing and learn what new farming techniques they had tried. Then the whole family would hit the midway with the rides and games, and before long they would all be laughing and having a great time. Kelly had the dreadful feeling that this was not going to be one of those times. "A trigger? How do we find something like that?"

"That's *your* job. You're supposed to know how to do that."

"Well, I don't," Kelly admitted, still looking fondly toward the sparkling lights.

"We'll figure it out," Tim injected flatly.

"Then get going. You don't have much time."

"*That* I know," Kelly said.

They bid the black silhouette good-bye and walked toward the carnival. With every step the music got louder and, since the sun had set, the lights became more inviting against the darkening countryside—tangled strings of sparkling diamonds against black velvet. Experiencing a sense of excitement, the two moved off a little faster.

"How'd you like to take a ride in that balloon?" Tim asked, indicating the red-, white-, and blue-starred balloon hovering even larger now.

"Yeah, right," Kelly said with weary sarcasm, "that's just what I want to do—add to my excitement. All we do is find what we have to find and get out of here. Uncle Morty's probably even in more trouble than before. Time keeps ticking away."

They'd gone about halfway again when a sound seemed to creep into their heads over the growing carnival sounds. A voice? Yes. A woman's. Where? From beyond a shallow hill. What was it saying? Calling something.

They stopped in their tracks.

"It's here—over here," the woman's voice said.

"What's over there?" Tim called back.

"It's here," the woman repeated.

Questions rattling in their brains, both kids turned and took a few steps around the hill. The lights from the carnival lit the area, but the back of the hill was cast in lengthy shadows. The voice came from those shadows.

# CHAPTER 13

Staring into the shadows from which the woman's voice came, Kelly whispered, "Can you see anything?"

"Nothing," Tim answered. He called out, "What have you got?" He took a few more steps toward the shadows.

"Don't leave me here," Kelly said and joined him.

"I can't just call it out," the woman said.

Kelly sighed. "We have to go back there, don't we?"

"Sure, why not?" Tim replied.

"Just remember the monkey," Kelly said.

The thought slowed Tim but didn't stop him. "Okay," he called softly to the voice. "We're coming."

"Look," Kelly pointed as they rounded the little hill. In the shadows was the dark silhouette of a woman. Her dress billowed slightly in the evening breeze as did wisps of her hair. "Next time we ask for flashlights," Kelly muttered.

Tim asked the woman, "What is it?"

The silhouette pointed to a boulder in the middle of a small clearing and spoke in a haunting whisper, "Touch that boulder and you'll be released from Virtual Reality."

"Released?" Kelly asked. "Like how?"

"Touch it and see."

"Just touch it? We don't have to carry it around with us or anything? Just touch it?"

"Why would you be doing this?" Kelly asked skeptically.

"What difference does it make?" Tim injected. "I'll go touch it and see."

Without hesitating, he walked toward the boulder. He only got about halfway. "Quicksand," he said with soft menace. He stopped, his shoes beginning to sink.

"Get out of there!" Kelly urged.

Tim tried to work his feet free so that he could escape, but the more he worked them the deeper they sank. "Get a limb or something. Help pull me out of here!"

Kelly glanced toward the shadowy woman. "She's gone!" Kelly exclaimed.

"Gone? A trap—and I got sucked right into it."

Without replying, Kelly looked around for something that might help. Not far away was the small grove of trees. She ran quickly to them and foraged around until she found a long limb. Running back with it, she stood on the edge of the quicksand and extended the limb toward Tim.

He reached out for it. "A few more inches."

Kelly looked down at her feet—a few more inches might be all it took to put her where Tim now found himself. But that really didn't matter. She had to do everything she could to help Tim.

She shuffled forward another six inches. Tim was only able to get a couple fingers on the branch. "A few more inches," he said again, his voice becoming more anxious.

Kelly took a quick breath. The ground on which she now stood was soft. It had already begun to close in around the soles of her shoes. Whoever had devised this little trap had done a good job.

"Okay, hang on," she said resolutely. Knowing what she had to do, she shuffled forward, pushing the limb out as far as she could.

Tim grabbed it and held tightly. "Pull me out of here!"

She might as well have been pulling a mammoth out of a tar pit. She put her whole weight into it, but except for his leaning toward her, Tim didn't budge.

The muck was up to his calves now, and every movement he made to work his legs free only worsened his position.

"This isn't working," Kelly called to him. "Now I'm sinking too."

"Maybe if you just fell backward onto firm ground—"

The instant the suggestion was made, Kelly did it. Her bottom planted on firm ground, she began to extract her legs. It worked. Within a minute or two the quicksand released her. "I'm out," she cried.

"Good," Tim said, his voice betraying worry about his own

situation. He was now up to his knees in the ooze. The only thing that could possibly help him now would be a crane.

"I don't know what to do, Tim," Kelly called to him. "Do you think that air will stop when you go under? Maybe I can find a longer limb or something. Should I run back and try to get that CIA guy to help?"

"Maybe he'll have a helicopter that can pull me out of here."

"Are you sure you want me to leave you?"

"Go find him. It's my only chance."

Reluctantly, Kelly got to her feet and ran to the pathway. Turning away from the carnival, she ran as fast as she could.

The slop was almost to Tim's waist by the time Kelly disappeared into the darkness. The suit simulated quicksand by making it a cool, undulating mass against his skin. Tim had no idea if quicksand really felt like that, but it didn't matter. If his head ever dipped below the surface, as Kelly had suggested, his air *would* probably stop. That's what mattered.

*This is serious*, Tim mused gravely. "Last time I just sank right through," he said, remembering when he and Barney were trying to elude Hammond Helbert the last time he was in VR. "Maybe that will happen this time."

He sank to his chest. Instinctively he used his arms to try to "swim" out. But that quickly proved to be of no use. "Where is she?" he asked the night, hoping he would see Kelly storming in from the path and hear the rhythmic throb of helicopter blades hovering overhead as it dropped him a line. Yet he saw no one and heard nothing but the irritatingly joyful carnival music.

His chin met the ooze now. In a last desperate effort, he kicked his feet and grabbed at the quicksand with his hands, but he only sank faster, if that were possible. He clamped his mouth tightly shut as the sand climbed to his VR visor. The earthen brown muck continued to rise until all shadows were gone—all light was obliterated and Tim was plunged into darkness. As his worst nightmare was realized, the air stopped.

Gulping the last bit of it, he managed to fill his lungs. How long could he last? A minute, maybe two. Would VR really allow him to not breathe? There just *had* to be a sensor that would turn the air back on in time.

But it didn't turn back on.

His lungs fought to keep the air in. They began to ache in his chest.

*How much longer? Oh, Lord, please, this can't be happening. You said you would take care of me. Never leave me nor forsake me. You're here in VR too.*

He had to breathe. He could feel his body telling his lungs to breathe. To take another gulp of air. But there was no air to gulp.

He began to thrash his body to fight for the surface. But the surface wouldn't come.

Until suddenly—the ooze that held him tightly, that encased his body like a vise, instantly became like water. It was as if he were in a pool.

Grabbing a handful of water, Tim propelled himself to the surface. His visor showed light and shadows again, and his air came back on, filling his helmet, then his lungs. No air had ever felt so wonderful, so pure and clean and fresh. He gulped, breathing deeply.

He heard Kelly shouting with joy, and seconds later he felt a limb falling on his shoulder. He grabbed it and Kelly easily pulled him to firm land. Without a moment's hesitation, Tim rolled onto the land and as far away from the quicksand as he could. Lying still for a moment, he continued to gasp for air until finally his body had its fill. Eyes focusing now, he saw Kelly kneeling beside him, her smile wide and welcoming, her eyes bathed in relief. "I couldn't find the guy, and when I ran back you were gone. I didn't know what to do. I prayed and prayed. Then you popped up. What happened?"

"It just turned to water," Tim said, words coming hard through his panting.

"Just rest for a minute. Just rest."

▣

Hammond laughed when he saw Tim sink into the ooze he'd created. The way he'd put the scene together by only changing the parameters was nothing less than genius. He had found a computer character, made her a shadow, placed her near a secluded patch of ground, put a boulder in the middle of it, and simply turned the solid ground around the boulder to ooze.

Then he crippled the complex interaction/dialogue module and wrote something simple and repetitive. And it worked the very first time. Drew the kids in and made them sweat. Maybe he *was* as smart as his brother.

Of course, when his brother, wherever he might be, interfered and changed the ooze to water, that was okay. Hammond really didn't want to kill the kids—at least not now. His laughter changed to a frown, but only for a moment.

The carnival was next and the CIA's silly games. Both presented Hammond with wonderful opportunities—they were made for what he wanted to do. If he moved quickly and used his imagination, he could easily outwit his brother.

*Those kids will never know what hit 'em.* "Good," he muttered to himself. "They're on their way again. Wonderful." He laughed again. "This is going to be fun."

◎

It took Tim most of the walk to the carnival to recover. It makes a deep impression when lungs cry out for air and there isn't any. What if the quicksand hadn't turned to water in time? Would VR have sensed that he was about to expire and turned the air back on, or would VR have let him die? Would God have let him die? Obviously not yet, for God, through whomever or whatever means, had allowed him to escape.

For all his thinking, though, it was Kelly who spoke first. "The quicksand was a trap," she said gravely. "And it was geared toward us. We're the only ones who would want to get out of the training. Anybody else would have to go through it no matter what."

"Our enemy again?"

"Makes a big monkey, makes quicksand, and draws us to both. Maybe he even made the meteor hit the space station. I doubt something that big would have been part of the training."

"But our friend, the guy who's looking out for us, took care of us—we escaped it all."

"Or the enemy let us escape."

"Either way," Tim said, "prayer seems to help."

They now stood before the carnival gate. Because finding the nuclear triggering mechanism would demand all their attention now, they stashed everything else in the back of their minds. They would think about the rest later.

"You folks coming in?" the scruffy barker at the gate called to them.

"Sure," Tim said, getting into character—a carnival patron.

"Come right on in," the carny greeted. "No admission. Just spend a lot of money while you're here."

Tim and Kelly stepped through the gate and melted into the milling crowd. People moved around them, some ignoring them, some coming close enough to bump into them, some crossing their paths, running from here to there. All in all it was a fun crowd, choruses of cheerful voices and laughter. A balloon vendor with a cloud of red, white, and blue balloons floating over his head crossed their path and continued on, several children following behind him. In spite of the seriousness of their mission, Tim and Kelly felt better being surrounded by happy, fun-loving people.

"This still could be a kick," Tim said.

"The rides maybe, but I've never won anything at these games."

"You don't have to win to have fun."

"I do," Kelly said flatly. "The games and sideshows are on the outside, and the rides are inside. They've got tents and booths here and there. Then there's that balloon out back. Where do you want to start first?"

"Let's just look around for a while. Maybe we'll see something that makes this easy."

"There's no map this time. Maybe the VR control room is in here too."

"I guess we'll see."

They meandered down the walkway that surrounded the carnival, games on both sides of it. Pitching dimes, horse racing with squirt guns, baseball throws—participants stood at each booth, some screaming, some taking serious aim, all having fun. The scene appeared very normal.

Suddenly a fight erupted.

Raised voices burst from two men, both dressed in slacks and colorful sports shirts, one at the baseball toss, the other at the basketball shoot—about twenty yards apart. Both men were large with broad shoulders, barrel chests, and meaty faces. They were shouting in a foreign language, and although the kids couldn't understand a word of what was said, there was little doubt that they were agitated. Each took measured steps toward the other, each step launching another verbal assault, another threatening flailing of arms. When about ten feet apart each could take the other's verbal assaults no longer. The guy by the baseball toss charged the other man. They slammed together like two trucks, and a moment later, fists flying, they rolled in the dirt.

A crowd gathered around, and as the men bucked and rolled about, the people made room for them, ebbing and flowing like a tide. Now and then the tide didn't flow fast enough, and a few people were mowed down.

"Shouldn't we get closer?" Tim asked. "It's got to be something to do with that trigger thing."

"People are falling like bowling pins. I'll stay right here," Kelly said.

As it turned out they didn't have to move.

Tim felt a nudge—shoulder to shoulder.

Tim turned to see a guy dressed much like the two combatants who were still battling at the center of the crowd—a sports shirt and slacks. The man's eyes were at half-mast, darting this way and that, like prey fearing the predator.

He asked in a rasping, gravely voice, "You CIA?"

"What?" Tim said.

"No games. I got what you want. You gotta hide me."

"Hide you where?"

"I don't care where. But you gotta hide me."

Kelly moved to the man's other side. "What have you got?"

"I know where it is." His eyes continued to bounce everywhere, his expression tight.

"Where is it?"

"Not 'til you hide me."

Tim thought for a moment. "I've got a place."

"Where?" The man was nearly beside himself.

"You tell us first."

He said nothing but slipped a small piece of paper into Tim's hand. "Now where?"

"Leave through the front gate, and when you get to a small hill on the right, go around behind the hill. Just stand near a boulder there for a while—you'll be hidden just fine."

"Great," the man said, no relief in his voice. "They're after me, and now they'll be after you."

Within seconds the man had disappeared beyond the games heading toward the front gate.

"How could you do that?" Kelly was shocked.

"He's a computer character—how can he stop breathing? And he'll certainly be hidden." As Tim spoke he unfolded the paper. There were only two words scrawled there in an uncertain hand: "It's floating." He handed it to Kelly.

"Floating? Where?" she asked.

The instant Kelly uttered "Where?" both sets of eyes went up to the large, red-, white-, and blue-starred balloon that hovered above the carnival and the gondola that hung below it.

"It's up there," Tim whispered, slipping the note in his pants pocket, his eyes glued to the gondola.

"How do we get to it?"

"Pull the balloon down or climb up the mooring rope."

"Not without being seen," Kelly argued.

"It's a shame we can't leap from a tall building or fly," Tim mused.

"Just wait a minute—knowing this place, it *could* happen."

Tim laughed. "Let's go see if there might be an easier way."

Remaining as casual as they could, they stepped past the grunting and rolling combatants and the crowd cheering them on, past several of the games and the carnies working them.

The carnies were thrilled when they saw Tim and Kelly ignoring the fight. "Need no skill," one called. "Great prizes," another one sang out. "Win your girlfriend a stuffed Dino."

Not to be sidetracked, the kids smiled at each other and continued.

They were, however, sidetracked by a gun. That's what Kelly suddenly felt in her side. "Don't turn," someone hissed.

She didn't.

"You neither," the voice growled at Tim. "What did that rat give you?"

"He didn't give me anything," Kelly said truthfully.

The man pushed the gun toward Tim. "I want it," he said.

"What?" Tim asked, exaggerating the puzzlement in his voice.

"I want what that guy gave you. I want it now." He sounded serious and jabbed the gun at them both again.

"What do you think a gunshot wound would do to you in VR?" Kelly whispered.

"Probably hurts," Tim said. "Are you going to shoot my sister?" he asked.

"It's my second choice. Hand over what he gave you. I'll count three, then I shoot." He didn't wait to begin. "One."

Kelly felt the gun jab her even harder. A bullet would never penetrate her in VR—nothing could do that. But the wound would definitely be excruciating; the electrified junction of the two wires in the suit at the point of impact would certainly burn deep.

"Two," said the man.

"Okay, okay." Tim's voice sounded as if he were crumbling.

Kelly had a different idea. Just as Tim pushed a hand into his pocket to retrieve the note, she spun, bent at the waist, and drove her shoulder into the man's midsection. Though not very big, she caught him by surprise. The gun was pushed aside, and her churning feet drove him off balance. While he struggled to regain his footing, Kelly cried out, "Tim. Go. Get out of here. I'll find you later."

With no time to determine if Kelly's command made sense or not, Tim reacted. There were rides on his left, games on his right, and the balloon straight ahead. He chose the rides. Saying nothing more, he launched himself to his left and scrambled past the ferris wheel and into the crowd of people milling in front of it. Only after he had successfully hidden himself among the crowd did he stop to think. He had left his sister with a gun-toting terrorist. Although the guy and the gun were virtual, the pain they could inflict was real.

A great brother he had turned out to be.

He decided to go back. Maybe he could still save the day, but at least he could give up the note and get his sister out of trouble.

When he got there, though, Kelly was gone. The fight had broken up, and people were now strolling around the games again. Accompanying the constant music was the sound of baseballs hitting wooden milk bottles, bells going off, dimes hitting little glass plates, and a siren or two.

But no Kelly.

Tim's heart sank. They had been separated, and he was responsible for whatever she was now enduring. He hated himself for leaving her. Brothers and sisters have to look out for one another. They were alone together in VR, and he had deserted her.

"Good job," Tim chided himself.

But he still knew the location of the bomb switch. If he delivered it to the shadowy CIA-guy then found the VR control room, he could set everybody free—including Kelly. He had to keep going. He had to get into that balloon gondola—somehow.

He started walking toward the balloon.

But after only a few steps, he noticed a man on his right in slacks and a flowered sports shirt standing at the corner of a game stall. Although the guy pretended to be ignoring Tim, Tim caught him glancing his way. In about a minute Tim would be even with him, and the guy would be on him like a fly.

Tim kept walking but glanced around. The rides again. He would have to duck back in there and try to lose himself in the crowd.

Taking another couple of steps, Tim prepared himself, then bolted to his left between two games toward the rides. Just as he was about to clear the back of the game stall a mountain of a man blocked his path—Tim could neither climb this mountain nor scamper around it. The mountain had been one of the men in the fight.

Tim was not only lanky, but agile. He skidded to a stop, spun, and tried to return to the main walkway. But another mountain appeared and blocked his escape. It was the other combatant. The second mountain pointed a threatening finger at the first mountain and shouted something at him. Although he spoke in that same foreign language, Tim knew exactly what he meant. He was saying, "Hands off him. He's mine, you scum." Tim was only guessing on the "you scum" part, but he felt sure about the rest. Especially when the second mountain brought his dangerously dark eyes back to him.

If he didn't act quickly, he'd be caught.

# CHAPTER 14

**T**rapped between two ominous mountains, Tim quickly identified his only escape route. The side of the game stall was tent fabric. Tim dropped to the ground, lifted the fabric, and scurried beneath it. *Big guys block well, but they don't move very fast*, he thought. On the other side of the canvas, he jumped to his feet and ran.

But he wasn't home free yet.

The first mountain didn't need to climb under the siding, he punched a knife through the top and slit it to the bottom, then stepped through to take up the chase. Although not as fast as Tim, he didn't have to be. Tim was confronted with another problem. He had unwittingly become part of a dart game. To his left was a wall of multi-colored balloons; to the right was a line of people throwing darts at them—sharp darts.

Tim dodged them as best he could. Fortunately, after a couple of darts scraped his skin, the people realized he was there and stopped throwing. The ones that hit him hurt—sharp jabs of pain. For a moment or two he ran unencumbered. Then he noticed the second mountain, which was running outside the game counter. Shoving the people aside, the man grabbed handful after handful of the darts and threw them at Tim as hard as he could.

Mountains throw darts hard. Fortunately, mountains can't aim worth beans. Now and then a dart hit him, and hurt severely when it did, but usually they flew harmlessly behind or ahead of him.

The game stall was only so long, though.

The mountain breathing down the back of Tim's neck gave him no time to dive below the approaching canvas wall, and with the other mountain pacing him and cutting off his only escape route over the counter, Tim wasn't quite sure what to do.

Only one choice presented itself. He grabbed a couple of darts, one in each hand, and prepared to hit the canvas at full speed. If the darts could start a little tear, the weight of his body slamming against it might open it up all the way.

Saying a quick prayer, Tim stabbed the canvas with the darts and immediately threw himself full force against it.

The instant his hand hit it the canvas became a thousand particles of confetti and vanished before him like smoke. Caught off balance, Tim stumbled slightly, but it didn't slow him down enough to matter. He turned a quick left and dove into the ride area. Within seconds he had moved into a small group of kids, wandered for a moment or two with them, then changed direction to a group of adults. Before long he had escaped the mountains. They were nowhere to be seen. He dove behind a protective tent flap, sat in the grass, and caught his breath for a second.

Tim was in good shape, but in the last few hours he'd gone through a lot. He needed to take a moment's rest—to regain his strength and prepare to get back in the battle. But where? Where would it be safe to take a break?

That's when he saw it. The Tunnel of Love.

Frank Holloway eyed a map of Maine. The high speed signal had been traced to a ground station just outside the Washington Beltway. It came there via a communications satellite and reached the satellite from a ground station in Bangor, Maine. From there things got a little fuzzy, but according to technicians in Bangor, the signal seemed to originate from somewhere about fifty miles northwest of there in a rugged part of the state.

Without hesitating, Frank phoned the Portsmouth FBI office, alerted them that he was coming, then boarded a Lear jet. Less than an hour later the jet's tires were squealing on the runway as it landed.

"There's not much out there," the FBI agent said when Frank joined him in a high-tech communications van.

"There doesn't have to be much—only one thing out there I care about," Frank told him.

"What's he done?"

"We just want him—badly. There will be presidential citations and bonuses all around."

"How many people do you want?"

"All of 'em."

"What are we looking for?"

"Someone out there is sending high speed data transmissions. Microwave—in the gigabyte range."

"Well, that shouldn't be too hard. What happens after we find 'im?"

"Hold him for me. No one else, just me."

The agent nodded and drove Frank to his office.

Years ago the Wisconsin State Fair had had a Tunnel of Love. Tim's mom and dad had talked about it. Small boats on a calm water channel slowly moving through a dark tunnel. It would be cool and private, and he could renew himself for just a few minutes. That's all he needed. While he was in there he could come up with a plan to get to that gondola.

He found ride tickets in his jacket pocket. He handed one to a ticket taker and stepped into one of the small boats. With the boat rocking gently, he glided into a cool darkness, the music fading along with his problems. Or at least they seemed to fade as the darkness closed in around him. He relaxed, so much so that he worried about falling asleep.

But then he thought about Kelly. How was she doing? Guilt boiled up. He shouldn't rest. He should be out looking for her—looking into every nook and cranny out there. But he couldn't very well get off the ride. He might as well get what he wanted out of it. Closing his eyes, he let the tension drain away.

Sometimes lately he felt so adult, as if all his decisions were well thought out and right, like he could do what needed to be done. But then there were times like these when he felt like a fourteen-year-old boy being asked to do something he wasn't prepared to do—and then he felt terribly inadequate.

Feeling emotionally drained, he thought, *It happened again.* He had been helped—the tent wall had disintegrated, letting him escape. He might not be prepared to do what was being asked of him, but at least he had some help—which only meant he *did* need help. He *was* inadequate.

"Tim."

Was someone calling his name? Was he dreaming? A girl's voice. Kelly's? No, too soft—velvety.

"Tim, I'm over here."

Breaking out of his sudden depression, Tim opened his eyes. He was still in the tunnel's deep shadows. Squinting, he strained to see who was speaking.

On a small walkway that ran along the right side of the waterway stood someone he had dreamed about, someone he had vowed not to care for again, someone who wasn't a *someone* at all—and yet was *someone* enough.

"Sonya," Tim whispered.

"Join me," she purred. "Up here. Climb out of the boat."

Heart pounding, Tim didn't hesitate. A moment later he stood beside her on the walkway, the empty boat continuing on without him.

Kelly's battle with the guy with the gun was short. He regained his balance, and before she could escape he brought the gun up and pushed it in her face. "This is loaded with a one-fifty-eight grain, thirty-eight," he hissed. "It'll do a lot of damage."

She believed him and froze.

When the man realized how he looked pointing a thirty-eight revolver at a teenage girl, he concealed the gun in his jacket pocket. "Come on," he said, "we got places to go."

The gun in his pocket pressing against her back, they wended their way through a meandering group of people. Suddenly Kelly saw a knot of five guys walking toward them. She tried to move out of their way, but they drifted, remaining in front of her and continuing to move in her direction. When she approached they parted, and when they came together, four of the five cleaved off her captor. Locking arms with him, they simply carried him off.

Kelly was left with the fifth guy.

And what a guy he was—maybe sixteen with sea green eyes and wavy black hair. Broad-shouldered, he wore jeans, a white T-shirt, and a worn leather jacket. "You okay?" he said, his eyes softly inviting.

"Uh—sure," she responded, lost in his eyes for a second. "But how did you—"

"You CIA?" he asked just above a whisper.

"Who are you?" Her brows knit—maybe he was beautiful in appearance only.

He slipped a hand into his jacket pocket and pulled out a card—a CIA ID—Brad Tucker. "We saw you were in trouble. Thought we'd help."

"Thanks," she said, her heart warming under his gaze. "But aren't you a little young for the CIA?"

"No," Brad said simply and smiled.

Kelly found herself drawn to his smile. More than endearing, it had an intriguing twinge of mischief in it. But when she remembered why she was there, she recoiled from it. "Umm! I've got a trigger to find," she said. "I've got to go."

"Trigger? You know where it is?"

She responded coyly, "Maybe—maybe not."

Brad Tucker laughed softly. "If anyone would know, I bet you would. You look like you're pretty good at this."

"Really?" Kelly said, liking the compliment and liking the attention even more.

Brad looked around as if trying to detect someone spying on them. "I was just wondering."

"What were you wondering?" Kelly asked, moving a step closer to him. He was at least a head taller than she, and she had to crane her neck to look into his ruggedly chiseled face.

"Maybe I could help."

"Help?" she cooed. "If I'm so good, why would I need your help?"

Brad took a step toward her. He placed his hands on each arm and gave her a squeeze. "Because two heads are better than one?"

*Oh, and what a head you have*, Kelly mused. "Brad, Brad, Brad," she purred, "why couldn't you have come along when I had time?" She laughed as she realized what she was doing. "I'm always badgering Tim because he can't keep his mind on what he's doing. And here I go—"

"Tim? Who's Tim?"

"You're a cartoon, you know."

Brad looked puzzled. "A what?"

"You're a cartoon, animation—you've got the most beautiful eyes I've ever seen and really great muscles, and those high cheekbones—" By the time she got to the cheekbones she was getting short of breath. "Do you know Sonya?" she asked.

"Who?"

"She's a 'toon too. Tim is just nuts about her. I've always wondered how he could possibly be attracted to a cartoon. Now I know. It's those eyes—" Again she felt a little short of breath. She wasn't sure why. He *was* just a cartoon, the result of a programmer's imagination, his speech the result of a very clever conversation formulation module. But he looked wonderful, and he said all the things she wanted to hear.

"Maybe you could help," she said.

"Then you know where it is?" Brad asked.

Kelly's instincts came alive. Something in that baritone voice sounded just a bit too anxious. Her heart sank.

"I'm not sure," she told him, her lips trembling with the untruth.

A gun appeared in Brad Tucker's hand, pointing at her heart—which instantly turned to lead. "But you do know, don't you? I must have given myself away somehow. Now we'll just have to get the information out of you another way."

"But why do you have to be so handsome? Why can't you look like Bobby Walker at the church? Instead you look a little like Bernie Freeman."

"Come on. I'm taking you somewhere—"

"You're taking me all right," Kelly mused, darkly pushing herself in the direction Brad Tucker had indicated—toward the fun house.

By the time they reached the fun house, Kelly had resigned herself to having been willingly fooled. She should have known. Why would one CIA-person offer to help another CIA-person whose test was to get through a situation unaided? But it was the eyes that had drawn her in. She wanted to believe what she wanted to believe, that's all there was to it. Now she'd have to pay.

The fun house was like any fun house—funny mirrors, strange slides, curious rooms that make you dizzy—people laughing, joking—fat people reveling in looking skinny, skinny people rubbing it in.

She entered, followed by the sea green eyes and the gun.

"There's a door at the end of the hall," Brad pointed out.

As they walked past the mirrors, she noticed that even when Brad Tucker's top was string skinny and his bottom ballooned, he looked good. There was definitely something wrong with her discernment. *You should never think somebody looks that good when he has a gun in your back,* she thought.

They reached the door and Tucker knocked a signal. A moment later the door opened a crack and an eye appeared. The eye satisfied, the door opened the rest of the way. For the first time becoming rough, Brad Tucker pushed Kelly inside and slammed the door behind them. He engaged the dead bolt and turned around.

"In there," Tucker said gruffly and gave her a not so gentle shove toward a door on the other side of the room.

Even before being shoved, Kelly had seen what there was to see—and she didn't like any of it. It was a small lounge with overstuffed chairs and sofas—all filled by about fifteen thugs. All were powerhouses with thick muscles, chiseled features, and predators' eyes wearing desert camouflage commando-type fatigue uniforms, shoulder and belt holsters, and Uzis; they all sat waiting, eyes drilling her as she walked past. Where a few minutes before she had been coyly flattered, now she was vulnerable and frightened.

"Inside—quick," Tucker growled, poking her hard with the gun.

Obediently, Kelly opened the door and stepped inside.

Tucker closed it behind them.

Kelly now faced a little guy in a dark suit behind a big desk. The guy looked up with black, obsidian eyes. They drilled into her.

"I'm sure she knows where it is," Brad Tucker told him.

The black eyes never left her. "Do you?" he asked her.

"What?"

"Where is it?"

"What?"

"Just a little background for you so you know we're serious.

A man we saw you talking to acquired—stole—what we want. He took a down payment for it, then refused to keep his word on the price. He created a bidding war, and when we protested he got scared. Now he's hidden it, and we want it. My trusted associate here—" the black eyes indicated Tucker, "—believes you know where it is. He is seldom wrong."

"I was sure wrong about him," Kelly said as an accusation. She saw Brad smile as if complimented.

"So," said the black eyes and dark suit, "where is it?"

"He *told* us nothing," Kelly stated flatly.

The guy slowly stood—he was short, and his eyes remained fixed on her. "We're running out of time. I guess we'll have to hurt you."

Kelly swallowed hard. "Hurt?"

"Can I do it?" Brad Tucker asked.

Glancing back, Kelly saw a hateful leer creep across Brad's face. Now his eyes looked anything but inviting.

"Here?" Kelly croaked. "In the fun house?"

"Of course," the man said. "We can hurt you anywhere. It's no big deal."

"How could you say hurting me is no big deal?" Kelly said, astonished.

"It's no big deal," he repeated

"It *is* a big deal—hurting me would be a very big deal. I don't want to be hurt."

"What do I care what you want? You don't care what I want," the man said impatiently.

"What do you want?" Kelly asked.

"What that guy told you."

"He didn't *tell* us anything."

"Please, can I hurt her now?" asked Brad, almost pleading for the pleasure.

Escape was her only hope. She couldn't tell them what she knew. Then they would get the triggering device, and she and Tim would be stuck in this place for another round. Yet there was nowhere to escape to. The only way out was through the room with the fifteen commandos in it, and even if she thought she could get through that room, Brad stood between her and the door.

She glanced around the room. It was a typical office—plaques on the walls, in-out baskets, a computer terminal, filing cabinets, a shelf with knickknacks on it. Nothing that would stop the beautiful Brad from doing what he was pleading to do.

That's when Brad took her hand. Just for an instant she thought his beauty and gentleness had returned. But then he pressed the gun barrel to her palm.

He was going to shoot her hand. So much for beauty and gentleness.

Some fun house this had turned out to be.

"I really don't want you to do this," Kelly said as calmly as she could—her insides a knot.

"Then what did he say?"

"He didn't *say* anything."

A light dawned in those black eyes. "What did he give you?"

Should she lie? Was there any time when it was right to lie? To save someone?

"He gave you something," the man went on. "A note? You were right, Bradley. She does know." His face twisted into a horrible grimace. "Now really hurt her. Both hands."

"Wait!" Kelly cried.

The man's eyes widened. "For what?"

"I'll tell you," she said, head down, feeling ashamed—after all, it was just pain.

"Go ahead."

"Take the gun away from my hand."

A nod from the guy and a disappointed Brad Tucker pulled the gun away.

"Now. Tell me."

"Okay, I'll—"

Suddenly Kelly looked toward the corner, screamed and pointed. As a reflex, both men turned. The instant their attention was deflected, Kelly bent down and grabbed Brad's leg and pulled it out from under him. He fell backward. His head bounced on the floor, stunning him. Kicking his gun hand, Kelly ran over his chest to the door. She opened it and bolted out. Darting past the commandos, she reached the exit door in a couple of quick steps. To prevent their pouncing on her any second, she turned toward the office she had just left and cried to the commandos the only word that came to mind. "Lipstick! Lipstick!" The commandos leaped to their feet and knotted their way into the little office to see what "Lipstick" meant.

Kelly grabbed the door handle and turned. Locked! She twisted it again, hoping that it was just stuck—then she remembered that Brad had bolted the door. By now the commandos were onto her little trick. She twisted the handle again. This time the knob—actually the whole fixture—turned. The door had become sawdust, falling in a heap at her feet.

Not letting her surprise slow her down, Kelly burst into the hallway. She heard the man shouting, "Get her—then hurt her."

Kelly darted through the fun house, dodging this person and that. Bursting outside she headed toward the most people—the rides. Before she had gone but a few steps, the commandos spilled from the fun house behind her.

She scurried into a crowd of teens then to another and another. Then she darted behind a small roller coaster and crouched there as the cars clattered by. She caught her breath while evaluating her escape. She still had a long way to go.

Three commandos milled around in front of the roller coaster. They moved a step or two, scanned the area, then moved again. They spoke to one another, looked some more, and, to her delight, moved on to the next ride.

After a relieved sigh, Kelly looked around for deeper cover. Deciding to stay put, she turned toward her ultimate goal—the big balloon and the gondola suspended beneath it.

How could she get up there? Maybe she *could* hang on to the mooring line and bring it down to her. She had to get to it and see.

But suddenly there was no time to think.

A cry of recognition came from behind her. Kelly spun to see, not twenty feet away, one of the commando's meaty fingers pointing right at her, while he called to the others. She was in trouble again.

# CHAPTER 15

Kelly jumped to her feet and darted back into the crowd, but this time the commandos weren't about to be lost quickly. They stormed in right after her. She heard protests as people were shoved out of the way no more than a step or two behind her. She expected to feel a muscular hand on her shoulder any second. Dipping and slithering from group to group, through this line and that, she heard the sounds of her pursuers begin to fade. Elated, she knew she was escaping again.

Or maybe not.

She burst from a knot of teens and found herself facing three commandos. Checking rides, they didn't recognize her at first; each glanced her way then turned away, but when they heard their comrades closing in on her from behind they looked again. This time they saw her. She hated triumphant smiles like that.

Where to go now?

No time to even think about it. The commandos in front lunged at her. Pinched between the two groups, she scooted off at a right angle. But that didn't help her much. She had been spotted. She ran faster, giving it all she had, but her legs were rubberizing and her lungs rasping. She had to find a place to hide.

But where?

She looked over her shoulder. At least ten of them were darting and dodging, their focus on her never wavering.

Her legs kept churning, nearing the Tunnel of Love.

The Tunnel of Love! Oh, if she could only duck in there. It would be so cool, and she could lie in the dark and recover. But they would surely see her, and then she'd be caught inside with no way out. No. Resting in the tunnel wasn't going to happen.

Suddenly a hand grabbed her by the neck and yanked her back. "It's over," an all too familiar voice growled. She was unceremoniously spun around and came face-to-face with Brad Tucker. With an expression that no longer held even a hint of beauty, he said, "Come on. The boss wants you."

◻

"Frank."

His name crackled over the radio.

"I'm here," Frank Holloway replied.

"We've got something."

"What?"

"There's a crude microwave station hidden in the trees out here. We must have flown over it five times before we finally saw it. It's not far from a lake where we can land."

"Any houses or cabins nearby?"

"That's where it all breaks down. There's nothing down there. Or at least nothing that we can see. We've used the infrared, but all we get are some deer and a few raccoons—nothing that looks like people-prints. But the forest is pretty thick; he could be hidden. I've sent a good-sized group in to take a tree-by-tree look."

"What's 'good-sized'?"

"All I got."

"When you find the house," Frank said into the mike, "or the cave, or whatever, just pinpoint it for me. Don't go in. Just get me as fast as you can."

◻

When Brad Tucker grabbed Kelly, commandos swarmed around forming a protective cloak. Then Brad gave her a commanding shove. "Back to the fun house," he ordered.

But for all his bluster, they walked no more than ten yards before things started happening. Since Kelly was surrounded by acres of muscles and broad shoulders, she didn't see it all, but she certainly heard it.

An angry voice exploded somewhere in front of them.

Angry voices responded.

The commandos around her began to separate, putting space between themselves—making themselves harder targets. Now she could see. Ten more commando-types stood before them— each every bit as muscular as her captors, and also spread out.

This confrontation was beginning to look like a western gun-fight—so far without the guns.

Fists went up, fingers pointed, fiery words rifled back and forth. A boiling point was reached. The second group charged. The commandos surrounding Kelly stood their ground, but only for a second. After a few thundering blows were struck, they cut and ran, the new group right on their tails.

A moment before, Kelly was afraid for her life. Now she stood alone—just outside the Tunnel of Love—relieved. After making sure they didn't care about her anymore, she turned, took a huge rejuvenating breath, and stepped up to the entrance. Presenting a ticket she found in her jacket pocket, she climbed into the next empty boat and floated into the darkness.

Morty had been watching Gar for a while now. The boy did little but stare at the ground and now and then play with a small stick he had found there. Morty's heart went out to him. The fourteen year old looked so lost and forlorn that Morty decided to say something. "If your mom were here right now . . . " he began.

Gar's head came up.

". . . what would you two do to keep from getting bored?"

Before Gar could reply, the president's mouse-face came up. He sat in his place at the junction of the two invisible walls. "What kind of question is that? That's all he needs is to be reminded of his mother."

"She'd tell me about some adventure she had," Gar said, ignoring his father. "There was always some time when she had gone through something similar to what we were going through then."

"What story would she tell now?" Morty asked.

Gar smiled. "I don't think she was about to be trampled by buffalo."

"But what were her other stories?"

"Telling your mother's stories isn't going to help us," the president insisted.

"Actually there was a time," Gar began, his eyes looking off somewhere for a moment while he gathered his thoughts. "She was on a picture-taking safari in Africa."

"I really don't want to hear about that," the president protested.

"She was just out of high school," Gar continued, his face growing illuminated. "The trip was like a graduation gift from her father. He was rich."

"Still is," the president said with a note a bitterness.

"There were four or five people on the safari. Some of the pictures Mom took are still hanging in my room. I sure hope I see them again."

"I hope I see them again too," his father grunted.

"Anyway, they had gone out looking for giraffe. There was supposed to be a herd of them near some watering hole, so they took a couple of Jeeps and went off looking for them. But they didn't find giraffe—"

"Sure they found giraffe," his father interrupted. "Where do you think those pictures of giraffe came from?"

"She told me they didn't find any."

"She didn't either. She told you they nearly didn't but came upon them on the way back after encountering the buffalo."

"She encountered buffalo—like these?" Morty asked, keeping his attention on Gar.

"I guess it doesn't matter about the giraffe. But when they came to the watering hole they found a small herd of buffalo—"

"Cape buffalo," the president corrected. "They aren't like these."

Gar nodded. "They look like bulls, sort of, with horns that come out of their heads like their hair was parted in the middle and then go out and up to a point. They're mean, and bullets bounce off their heads when they charge."

"Did one of them charge?" Morty asked.

"Two of them did. One was shot by one of the guides."

"What about the other one?"

"Mom took a picture of it. She stood her ground—actually she was in a Jeep, but she waited until the last minute and took the picture. Then the Jeep driver gunned it and they got out of there."

"She sounds like a courageous woman," Morty said admiringly.

"And if she hadn't been so courageous, she'd still be here," the president said, his voice a mixture of anger and sadness. "She could do some dumb things sometimes."

"Mom wasn't dumb!" Gar fired back.

"If she was so smart, why didn't she hold on to that white-water raft? Why did she allow herself to be thrown out and hit that rock? Dumb—taking dumb chances. There's a lot of her in you—a lot."

"Don't you ever get tired of tearing each other apart?" Morty asked, his heart heavy. "Satan can hardly wait to drive a wedge between you. It's brilliant of him to use the memories of someone you both love to do it."

Their little prison fell silent again.

回

A half hour before Kelly had entered the Tunnel of Love, Tim first heard Sonya's velvety voice. A few minutes later he was led down the tunnel walkway to a small room—a plush sitting room. Sonya looked as beautiful as ever—maybe more. Her raven hair glistened, and her almond eyes seemed so deep he could swim in them.

"You look tired," she purred when they were alone in the room with the door closed behind them.

"It's been a wild few hours," Tim confided.

"You can rest here," Sonya cooed, offering an overstuffed chair.

"Here? With you?"

She smiled her velveteen smile and ran a hand up his arm to his shoulder. Warmth accompanied it. "Sit. This one's a re-cliner—I use it. It's comfortable. You can close your eyes for a while. Then we can talk."

"Talk?"

"A long conversation." Her lips caressed the word *conversation* like a kiss. Sonya knew her way around words—she knew how to use them like no one else.

Tim loved it.

He slipped into the recliner and leaned back—he sank into it, his head deep in the pillow as it reclined and the footrest rose.

"Close your eyes," she said softly as she stood behind him and rubbed his temples. "I'll be here when you wake. You look so tired."

"Even if I wasn't tired I'd like this," Tim crooned as his eyes closed.

Suddenly four iron cuffs snapped around his wrists and ankles, holding him tight. He was a captive.

"What's going on?" he exclaimed, trying desperately to squirm free. After several anxious moments, he had to give up. He looked up at his beautiful captor. "Did you do this?" He hoped she'd say no.

She shook her beautiful head. "Not me."

Tim's brows dipped and he pulled at the restraints. "Then who did?"

Sonya had no time to answer. A knock came at the door. She opened it to find an elf with pointy ears, pointy shoes, and steel black eyes. The elf stepped past Sonya toward Tim. Without smiling, he said, "I caught your uncle, and now I have you. Only that Kelly girl to go." Hammond Helbert laughed—the kind of laugh that sent a bullet of terror racing up Tim's spine.

Wrists and ankles beginning to chafe, Tim demanded, "Who are you?"

The elf's eyes narrowed. "Just call me 'sir.'"

Tim again tugged at his restraints. "Yeah—right. What's all this about?"

"Hurting *you*." Another hateful grin.

"Me? Why me?" That's when it all came together. "You must be Hammond Helbert—Matthew's brother!"

"No. Matthew is *my* brother."

"Big difference."

"It *is* a big one. He's the good genius. I'm the rich one—or I will be rich when this is over. You, your uncle, and that sister of yours will be in the hospital or the grave, and I'll be rich. They'll pay well for a president, then the president will pay for his son. I love a good bargain. But first I deal with you."

"What are you going to do to him?" Sonya asked.

Tim heard a hint of challenge in her voice.

"What's it to you?" Hammond Helbert growled at her.

"He's a friend," she said cautiously.

"You can be erased, you know. Or turned old and frumpy. How'd you like every one of those long, beautiful nails to break—every day—grow, break, grow, break. You want that? I can do it."

"My nails? I love my nails."

The elf shook his head, the end of his tolerance having been reached. "Computer characters—Matthew was too lonely when he created all of you—he needed a life." Hammond looked up to the ceiling, then at the walls. "Did you hear that, Matthew? Save him this time if you can."

"Has Matthew been helping us?" Tim asked, hoping to finally answer the question that he had been asking himself.

The elf became uncharacteristically thoughtful for an instant. "I think so," he said. Then thoughtfulness vanished and hard, gray steel returned to his eyes. "Remember the thorns?"

Tim remembered. The last time he and Kelly were in VR they'd had to get through a sea of them—long and sharp and waiting to sting. Even now, sitting in the comfortable chair, he relived the electric shock—the stab of the thorn—on his leg where wires in the suit crossed. It hurt. He had no desire to meet those thorns again.

"What about them?" he asked.

The elf smiled. Across the room from Tim was a wardrobe—an ornately carved floor-to-ceiling cupboard in which one would normally hang clothes. The elf stepped over to it and opened both doors.

There were no clothes in the wardrobe.

There were thorns—hundreds of them—those same long, saber-like thorns that had introduced themselves to Tim so painfully before. A crisscross of them protruded from the back of the wardrobe and from the doors. When the doors were closed they would cross, leaving no room for even a rabbit in there.

"I'm going in there?" Tim gasped.

"You're going to put him in *there*?" Sonya gasped too. "He's real. He will be hurt."

The elf ignored her, his level eyes steady on Tim. "You beat me last time. You, that uncle of yours, and your sister tore millions of dollars out of my hands. No one does that to me and gets away with it. After a few minutes in there, you'll not only wish you hadn't done that the first time; you'll make sure you never do it again—if you're ever able to do anything again. I really have no idea what the VR suit will do when asked to simulate all those thorns digging into you—maybe going all the way through you. Not only did Matthew try to make things realistic, but those CIA people, aided by me, tried to improve it. They were artists."

"You can't do that to him," Sonya protested.

"Sure, I can."

"What if I refuse to go?" Tim said.

The elf only smiled, brought up a small device about the size of a lighter, and sprayed him. The instant he did, Tim smelled something wafting up from the base of his helmet—something he might smell in a doctor's office. "What's this suit doing to me now?" he groaned. A second or two later, everything went black.

Frank Holloway sat in the passenger seat of an FBI communications van. Parked along the highway in south-central Maine, he listened intently to the reports from several search teams coming in to the wall of communications gear behind him. They were looking for the hole Hammond Helbert was hiding in.

They had to find him quickly. The pressure was on.

A few hours earlier Terry Baker had contacted Frank. His voice had sounded agitated, unusual for Baker. The vice president had stumbled upon the Virtual Reality machine room in the White House basement while looking for the president. When he saw what was going on, he'd insisted that Baker tell him everything.

"He went ballistic," Baker had told Frank. "I respect the man, but he gets so emotional. Kept asking what he would do if war broke out or someone ordered a missile strike. You've got to get the president out of there."

Now Frank waited anxiously for a search team to find what it was looking for.

"Alpha to base, over," came a crackling voice.

"Base here, over," the communications specialist behind Frank replied.

"We found him!"

Frank Holloway nearly cheered and grabbed a mike that rested on the dashboard. "Where is he?"

"Under a massive oak tree. The equipment says he's really dug in. It's a neat place—lake nearby. When we put him away I might buy the place for fishing."

"We gotta catch him first. Can you see him in there?"

"We've got him on the infrared. But he's got a fence all around the place, and we don't want to risk alerting him."

"At least you're thinking."

The man on the other end of the line laughed. "I'm always thinking. If you ever get here, I guess we'll see what kind of thinking you do."

"I'll get there. Just make sure you're ready when I do."

"We'll send a chopper for you. After you land you'll need to travel here by Jeep. Might be a little bumpy."

"Just stay out of sight 'til I get there. We've got to capture this guy. If he gets away, we're in deep weeds."

Tim wasn't sure how long he'd been unconscious. He only knew he was awake now, and his head hurt. After a moment or two his senses cleared and he realized something else. His hands were tied to the wardrobe's inside ceiling, and the thorns were pricking his back. The doors were still open, the elf and his evil grin of anticipation stood before him.

"Where's Sonya?" Tim asked.

"She had other things to do. One of them was keeping her mouth shut."

"What happens now?"

The elf smiled broadly. "I wanted to wait until you were conscious. It only hurts when you're conscious."

"Can I take a minute and pray first?" Tim asked.

"No," said the elf.

Tim did pray—a quick, frightened prayer.

"Well," the elf sneered, "have a wonderful day."

Without another word, Hammond Helbert shut the two doors on Tim.

When the doors were nearly closed, Tim began to scream. A high-pitched, awful scream that Hammond Helbert loved—a truly wonderful sound to this particular elf's ears. It was so wonderful that Hammond Helbert decided to give the doors a little extra push. He fell against them in a final shove. Tim screamed even louder—as if boiling with pain.

Thrilled with his half hour's work, Hammond Helbert locked the doors and slipped out of the office. Finding the programmer's entry/exit point on the carnival's perimeter—one he had placed there himself so that he might move quickly between the various Virtual lands—he stepped through it, returning to the western town.

*Why did I make this place so hot and dusty?* he thought as he sat down at the saloon table. *Next time I'm here I'll figure out a way to get a drink in VR. I'm thirsty. But first things first,* he said to himself. *Now that I've heaped my vengeance on that boy creep, it's time to figure out how to pile it onto the girl creep.* He laughed heartily. *Maybe I could do something with that balloon—yes, that would be nice—falls from great heights can be excruciating.*

◻

Kelly had been floating in the Tunnel of Love for only a few minutes. She'd actually rested for a moment and closed her eyes to let the darkness envelop her. But then her ears perked.

Screams?

It sounded like screams. It was hard to tell because of the muffled music and the sound of kids laughing and screaming outside. But the kids' screams were different—happy, excited. The scream she heard now was charged with pain.

Was it Tim?

It came again. This time ending in a muffled, mournful whimper.

Kelly wasted no time. She rose up, balanced herself on the boat as best she could, and leaped onto the walkway.

"Hey," someone called from a boat in back. "What are you doing?"

She paid no attention but ran quickly to where she thought the screams were coming from. But they had stopped now. In the darkness she could see nothing but the phony rock that lined the tunnel.

"He's in here," came a voice—an ancient woman's voice.

In the dim shadows Kelly saw the woman's bent figure standing a few feet away. "Tim?"

"It was horrible," the old woman said.

She led Kelly into the sitting room and pointed at the wardrobe. "He's in there," she said, her voice betraying the horror of what would be found inside. "Thorns," she whispered.

Kelly groaned as she approached it. "It's locked," she said after trying the doors. "Oh, Lord—what has happened to him?"

# CHAPTER 16

Kelly?" Tim's voice came from inside the ancient wardrobe.

While Kelly stood before it, the old woman looked about the room. A key lay on a small end table. Before the old woman could get to it, Kelly grabbed it and unlocked the doors. Tim burst out, a smile of recognition spread all over his face.

Kelly registered shock. There were no wounds on him at all.

"You're not hurt!" she exclaimed, untying his hands.

Tim laughed. He turned back to the wardrobe and twanged one of the ugly thorns. "Rubber," he said and laughed again. "I couldn't believe it. When the door closed they just bent."

The old woman also registered shock. "I tried to fight him off," she said, her voice ancient and strained. She took a wrinkled hand and touched one of the thorns. "Rubber." She turned toward Tim. "You're safe."

Tim looked at the old woman for a moment. Although he didn't recognize her face—it was sagging and wrinkled, void of color—he did recognize the eyes. They were unchanged—deep and almond colored, full of life. "Sonya?"

"Sonya?" Kelly echoed in disbelief.

"He did this to you?" Tim asked.

"He changed my characteristics," she cried, bursting into tears.

Kelly turned back to her brother in confusion. "But I heard you screaming out in the tunnel."

"I had to. The moment I got in there I knew the thorns wouldn't hurt me. Our friend helped me again, but I couldn't let Hammond Helbert know that."

"He was here?"

"As an elf. He's a bit upset with us. I think he's got Uncle Morty and the president and his son held captive someplace. But he also thinks Matthew Helbert is the one helping us."

"He helped me again too. A door disintegrated and let me escape from a bunch of commandos."

"You were chased?"

"All over the place."

"Me too. That's why I came in here."

"We still don't have much time."

"I'll be leaving now," came Sonya's voice.

Tim was suddenly wracked with guilt. "I'm sorry," he said. "We just have this problem we have to solve, and it's a tough one. I'm sorry this happened to you."

Sonya, her back bent, her eyes cast to the floor, her youth history, nodded and shuffled toward the door. "I hope I see you again sometime, Tim. I've always liked you."

"How can a cartoon like anything?" Kelly asked.

Tim had a hard time saying this to someone—or something—who was now old enough to be his grandmother, but he said it anyway, "I've thought about you a lot too."

"Good-bye, Tim."

"See you."

Sonya gave a weak wave and disappeared out the door.

"She's a 'toon, Tim," Kelly said with an edge to her voice. But she thought of her first reaction to Brad's eyes and her expression softened.

"She gave up something for me—maybe VR characters feel things emotionally. We don't know."

"We can think about that later. We have to get that triggering mechanism and save Uncle Morty."

"Any ideas?"

"I left the terrorist groups battling one another outside. Maybe they'll be too busy to notice us. We can climb that mooring rope—or maybe even pull the balloon down."

Renewed, Tim and Kelly left the room and the darkness of the tunnel. The carnival lights seemed brighter and more cheerful somehow, the music more uplifting. Having a plan helped. Since the Tunnel of Love was built against the back fence, they merely followed the fence to the balloon. When they arrived their hearts were racing.

There were actually two mooring lines, two thick ropes anchored to the ground by two heavy iron spikes and held taut by the balloon's desire for freedom. The gondola was more than fifteen feet above the ground—maybe twenty-five—and it moved to the gentle rhythms of the night breezes.

Without hesitation, Tim grabbed one of the lines and pulled. The balloon refused to descend at all. Kelly grabbed the other rope and they both pulled. The balloon stubbornly remained aloft.

"We'll have to climb it," Tim said.

"You climbed a rope in gym, right?"

Tim nodded, looking up at the balloon again. "Keep a lookout."

Kelly nodded.

Tim grabbed the rope, took a deep preparatory breath, then launched himself. He *had* climbed a rope in gym, but it was a thinner rope, one he could wrap around his hand and get a good grip on. This was a thick, unyielding rope, and the climb was more difficult. But he had to succeed and that was that.

After making sure Tim was on his way, Kelly turned. Her eyes acting like search lights, they swept the midway, the rides and games, and the people. No terrorists. At least not at first; then she saw a couple of them scuffling near a game.

She glanced up at Tim. He was a little over halfway now, maybe fifteen feet high, his hands and feet working the rope, grappling for every inch. She could hear him grunting with each movement.

She turned back to her lookout. But she didn't have to work at it at all. Standing right before her was a bulky terrorist. There was no chance to warn Tim. A hand grabbed her by the jacket and all but lifted her off her feet; another hand clapped over her mouth, covering the lower edge of her VR visor.

Another commando appeared, then another. These two concentrated on Tim.

Kelly tried to cry out to him, but her voice was dead—the VR suit was gagging her.

Within seconds at least ten commandos crowded around, all staring up at Tim.

"It must be up there," one of them said.

"They thought they could get it away from us."

Suddenly one of them, then two, then three, lifted their Uzis.

Kelly wrenched away from the hand over her mouth. "Watch out, Tim!" she shouted.

Too late. They fired. But not at Tim—at the balloon.

The bullets tore huge, ragged holes in the balloon's fabric. The fabric began to flap frantically as the balloon lost altitude.

Tim cringed when more bullets whizzed by him. The rope was growing slack, and he found it more difficult to hang on.

The remaining pressure in the balloon tore it further, and it fell rapidly. Unable to hold on, Tim dropped to the ground. Fortunately he wasn't quite so high as before and landed easily. The instant he did he rolled and darted to the sidelines. No one paid attention to him.

All eyes were on the gondola. It dropped with the balloon and forty hands reached up to guide it to the ground.

Kelly noticed that the number of commandos had doubled. Both commando groups now crowded around the gondola. She also noted that none of the original commandos realized their ranks had swelled at first. But their ignorance lasted only a moment or two. Suddenly angry words began firing back and forth. Hands fought to dislodge other hands from the gondola, and when all the angry words and the grabbing failed, fists began to fly.

Kelly took Tim's outstretched hand, and they eased themselves away. Although glad for the opportunity to escape, they were depressed. The terrorists would get the triggering device, and they would be stuck in this place for another go-around.

Feeling the weight of the world on their shoulders, Tim and Kelly moved away from the battle to a bench near the carnival entrance and sat for a moment.

▣

Hammond Helbert slammed his fist onto the table. He'd seen it all. There was nothing wrong with that boy-creep. Nobody crushed by those thorns could have run and climbed like that. Matthew must have saved him again. *That does it—no more mister nice guy.*

That's when the alarm went off.

It was a real one. It rang in VR because Hammond Helbert had rigged it that way. It actually rang in his basement laboratory where he now sat in his own black VR suit. It meant someone had breached his real perimeter fence that protected his real laboratory.

Part of his plan to capture the president by turning off the palm escape buttons was to rig a personal escape button on his right wrist. He used that now. The instant he pressed it his visor came up and the suit went slack. He climbed out of it and stepped over to a wall of TV monitors. Three of them revealed the problem. Secret Service and FBI agents were pushing through the fence. Hammond could see the large letters on their backs from the cameras focusing in on them from beyond the perimeter. They'd found him. They would be at his cabin in less than ten minutes. He had anticipated this.

And he couldn't allow them to interfere with his vengeance.

Returning to his VR suit, he climbed in and zipped and helmeted himself. He used his small monitor to enter the address of the VR control room and jump to it. He instantly found himself in a circular room with every inch of wall space covered with various switches and monitors. His first act was to set a ten-minute timer—when the timer went off, ten minutes from now, the buffalo herd would be freed to trample his captives. Then he changed the characteristics of the transparent walls holding the president, his son, and the pesky uncle. They would continue to keep the captives in, but would now let people walk through from the other side—it would be a one-way door—a trap. *Come in and never get out,* he mused. Then he punched in a code—Tim and Kelly's code.

◘

Sitting on the bench, feeling like the world was about to come to an end, Tim and Kelly both heard Hammond Helbert's voice coming from inside their helmets.

"Hello, you two. This is your old friend, Hammond."

"Where are you?" they asked together.

"Don't say anything. You don't have time. You have ten minutes—see the little digital timer on the lower corner of your visors?"

The timer appeared. It read 9:58 and counting down.

"In that time, unless you come to rescue them, your uncle, the president of the United States, and that kid of his will be crushed by rampaging buffalo. It will make quite a mess. You would like to rescue them, wouldn't you? Sure, you would. You can, you know. Easily. All you have to do is find them and touch them—both of you—anywhere—hand, leg—anywhere. Then everyone will be released from Virtual Reality. Of course, if you're late—well, such is life. To find them, go to the carnival fence in back of the basketball toss. Grab the fence, and you'll find yourself in a western town. There will be horses waiting for you. They'll take you to your uncle."

The visor clock read 9:43.

"What if we don't?" Tim asked.

"Then you'll be responsible for killing the president, your uncle, and the president's kid. Well, maybe not killing, but hurting them *real* bad. I just hope none of them has a heart condition—then maybe they will die. I have to go now. Don't fail them. You won't like yourselves if you do."

Hammond Helbert then led the virtual horses to the hitching post outside the saloon and tied them there. Punching an address into his little terminal, he was instantly transported to the VR control room again. He found the switch he wanted, the one that allowed external transmission to VR—the kind of transmission that brought him and probably Matthew to VR—and flipped it off. VR went dark. "Okay, Matthew, you're locked out too. Now they're on their own in there." He then pressed his wrist button.

A moment later he climbed out of his black suit. He packed it in a small suitcase, threw in some other essentials, and headed for the door. He turned and looked at his laboratory with a sentimental fondness. "I'll be back soon," he said. From a jacket pocket he took a small black box that looked much like a TV remote control and pressed a button on it. That instant, the floor all around him began to drop until the top of the tallest cabinet was now below the level where the floor had been. He pressed another button, and another new floor moved in from either side wall. It came together seamlessly in the center. His work would be safe now—buried beneath wood and lead until he returned.

Sensing that he had only a minute or two left, he spun around, opened the door, and ran into an earthen tunnel beyond. The Secret Service and FBI were just behind him now, and he had a lot of ground to cover. Flipping on the lights, he quickly made his way to a maze of smaller tunnels, the path through which only he knew.

Kelly and Tim stared at the clocks in their visors. They ticked away like a fuse sparking toward dynamite.

"We have to go," Kelly said.

"He's lying," Tim said with true resolve.

"About the ten minutes?"

"No, I think he's telling the truth about that. But about us touching them. The only thing that will get them—and us—out is to get to that control room and reactivate the escape buttons."

"But we can't get there. What about the trigger? The terrorists will get the triggering device, and we'll have to go through this again."

Then they saw something unexpected. A remnant of the two terrorist groups burst into view toward the rear of the carnival—they were no longer fighting but were shouting angry, dejected words back and forth.

"They didn't find it," Kelly said. "It wasn't in the balloon gondola."

"They'd still be battling if it was."

A new thought crept into both their heads.

The balloon vendor stepped onto the midway and began walking toward them.

"It's floating," they said in unison, remembering the spy's note.

"It's worth a shot," Tim said.

"But the triggering device has to be heavy," Kelly questioned.

"This is VR. It's as heavy as the programmer makes it."

Tim leaped to his feet, ran to the dart game, and grabbed a dart. Seconds later he was standing before a shocked balloon vendor aiming at the balloons. The pops occurred rapidly. After he hit several, a metal cylinder bounced off the vendor's head and fell at Tim's feet.

With a squeal of delight, Kelly grabbed the cylinder while Tim threw a handful of money he found in his jacket at the vendor. They both ran for the carnival exit.

▣

Frank pushed a phone to his ear and dialed Terry Baker's number.

"Baker," came the voice.

"He got away. At least for now."

"I didn't want to hear that. Are you after him?"

"He's gone into a cave, and there's probably twenty smaller caves leading from it. I've put a helicopter in the air with an infrared monitor. If he's underground we won't find him."

"What are we going to do?"

"Get the president's doctor—we might have to cut him out of there. Find out what we can do to lessen the chance that he dies." Frank hesitated then continued, "Call Murphy, the head of the Secret Service; all this is his responsibility anyway. He can make the decisions. With the doctor there and Murphy's okay you might be able to cut him out in a few minutes."

"I'll make the decision. But getting him out of there is our only hope."

"Well, that's your call, but from what I know of the president's condition, the doctor's presence probably won't help."

Terry only nodded. He had a difficult decision to make.

"Hey!" A voice called to Tim and Kelly from the wooded shadows.

The call caught them mid-stride. They turned to see the dark silhouette who had given them their assignment standing there.

"We got it. We got it," they both called in unison. Seconds later Kelly handed it to him. Their visor clocks read 7:58.

"We gotta get out of here," Kelly told him anxiously.

"There's usually a ceremony."

"We don't have time for a ceremony," Tim said. "We've got to go."

"No ceremony?"

"We want out!" insisted Kelly.

"Well, okay," the shadow said, a little frustrated, head bobbing in disbelief. But, giving in to their demands, the shadowy figure snapped his fingers.

That moment their world went black. The only thing they saw was the clock: 7:45.

Uncle Morty was going stir crazy. Nothing had been said between father and son since Gar's story about the Cape buffalo and the president's callous reaction. But though they'd been silent, the tension was electric—the current all but unbearable for Morty.

He had to get out of there. Yet the Lord had locked him in with these two as surely as if he'd turned the key himself.

Would they ever get out? Were Tim and Kelly also locked up awaiting execution?

To relieve some of the strain, he slammed his fist against a buffalo head. It was like hitting a boulder. There was a time when he thought buffalo were noble beasts, beautiful in their own way, but not now. After staring endlessly at a whole wall of them he found them remarkably ugly. Especially the way they were frozen mid-stride—eyes black like marbles, lips apart gasping for air, fur flying back. Any second they might come to life and trample the three of them. Uncle Morty found himself partly wishing it would happen. At least it would break the tension and bring things to a head.

He found himself praying again. It was the same prayer he'd prayed before—for their rescue, for strength if they had to go through whatever VR handed them when they were being trampled. He ended by asking the Lord to get on with his plan—whatever that was.

The instant the prayer ended he heard the president say: "Your mom and I met on that camera safari."

Surprised by the sudden sound, Morty eyed Gar for his reaction. His head came up. "It hurts to think about that safari since she died."

There was a softness in the president's voice as if his anger had been left behind somewhere. "It was right after the Cape buffalo incident. She was still excited about it—alive with the experience. I think I fell in love with her right then. I was in college and doing some research on the African tribal system, so we only met for a moment or two. I looked her up again when we were back in the States. She was an exciting woman."

As if afraid to break his father's mood, Gar only nodded.

"When you came along, though, she slowed down. She wanted to be a good mother to you, to spend a lot of time with you. And—she always wanted me to spend more time with you too. She wanted me to be a good father."

"That would have been okay," Gar ventured hesitantly.

"She kept saying that God gave us a baby boy and boys need their fathers. She would read the Bible to me about my responsibilities to you before God." He fell silent again as if wrestling with regret. "I was saved in high school," he went on. "Even though we met for such a short time in Africa that first time, she somehow found that out. She seemed glad that I was saved. We went out all through college, then got married. I wanted to go into politics, and she wanted to have children. She saw them—you, really—as her greatest adventure."

He was on his feet now, pacing, trying to put words together. "I waited a long time to have kids, and when you came, even though I was as thrilled as any father would be, I saw that you could get in the way of my ambitions. I'd just realized I could make it to the top—to the presidency. If I did spend the kind of time with you she wanted, I wouldn't be able to spend the time necessary to get to the White House. So—I all but abandoned you to her. And then she died—I resented it. Not only had I lost the love of my life to an accident she could have prevented, but now I had to be a father, and I didn't want to be one."

The president's mouse face came up, his mouse eyes apologetic. He looked at Morty first. "When you said that about Satan, it started me thinking. At first I rejected that Satan could ever do anything in my life. Then I realized I'd been playing right into his hands all along. I've been letting my ambitions destroy what God had given me." Now he turned to his son. "I've been horrible to you, son. I've been horrible to God. Jesus died for me, and when he gave you to me as a gift I all but threw you back at him. Forgive me, son. Please. I love you so."

Gar didn't know what to say. This was a new father saying these things. "Sure, Dad," he said, self-consciously. With a deeply serious expression, he said, "Dad, I'm sorry I got you into this."

"In one sense it is a horrible thing to happen to the president of the United States. But in a far better sense, it is the best thing that could have happened to us." He walked over to his son, and when Gar was on his feet, President Harkin wrapped longing arms around his son. "God is even here in Virtual Reality," the president said.

Morty nodded, then eyed the rigid wall of buffalo. "That's what I'm counting on," he said.

## CHAPTER 17

I can't believe this," Tim groaned as he stood before a worn wooden door in a huge brick wall. The wall stretched forever in all directions—right, left, up. "Haven't we been here before?" He tried the ornate brass handle. It jiggled but refused to give way.

Kelly stood beside him. She, too, groaned. "We're going to turn around now and I know what we'll see."

They did turn, and it was just what they expected—the canopy of thorns eight feet above their heads. It was all there like the last time they were in VR, the vines intertwined, the shadows beneath the canopy, the occasional trunks reaching from the thorns to the ground. The thorns clattered above them menacingly.

The visor clock read 7:12 and was dropping fast.

"Tim, look," Kelly said, bending over and picking up a scrap of paper on the ground. "It's a map." She positioned it so Tim could see it too.

It was quickly and crudely drawn, but it said it all.

"This is the canopy of thorns," Tim said, pointing to a series of crisscross lines.

"Here's the control room," Kelly said, pointing to a labeled circle just beyond a scrawled river just beyond the thorns.

"We've got less than seven minutes, and there's a long way to go."

Kelly glanced up. "When we walk under the thorns we lose gravity and float up toward them," she remembered.

"Remember the snakes?"

"Like I could forget snakes," Kelly whispered. "There have been far too many snakes this time around." Snakes with yellow eyes and sleek, slithering bodies made the thorns their home. Tim had been bitten by one on their last trip too, and when he mentioned them his eyes had a look of dread.

"We ought to go over the top like we did last time."

"Right. Over the top."

Like a pro, Tim took a single step beneath the shadowy canopy. The moment he did, he floated up toward the thorns. When he reached them, he grabbed one in each hand and allowed his legs to dock gently between a couple of others. One of them stuck him, but only slightly.

Kelly followed. She, too, floated up to the thorns and deftly grabbed a couple, but instead of bringing her legs up to the thorns, she quickly began walking her hands from thorn to thorn up the edge of the thicket. She reached the top of the thicket before Tim.

Together they looked out over the sea of daggers. Nothing had changed; all the dangers were still there, and all the reasons to move slowly and with great care were still there. Of course, there was no time for any of that. They had to move quickly. If they got scratched up they would just have to take it.

After a single breath and a quick prayer for courage, they set out.

Their visor clocks read 6:05.

At first the going was difficult. Their rhythm was off. They would grab a thorn and miss, or lose their grip and drift. In the early going the thorns dug into them. The pinpoint electric shocks were painful, some more than others, but all caused them to hesitate for a moment, to slow down and take it easier. When they slowed, the clock seemed to tick faster.

"I see a snake," Kelly announced. Its sleek, dark body stretched out, then coiled around the vines and thorns on the interior of the thicket. When she moved past the head, the hypnotic yellow eyes glanced up at her. But the head didn't move.

They passed another snake. Again the head didn't move.

"Maybe we're going too fast for them," Tim said.

"Ouch!" Kelly felt another stab. This time she consciously kept her speed. A full minute had gone by and another was about to disappear. They were making good progress, but the field of thorns didn't seem any shorter. "It's never going to end," she moaned.

"It does. Believe me. You never saw the whole thicket, did you?" Tim responded.

"I floated off."

"The problem is we float to the sky when we do get to the end. We'll just have to figure out what to do when we get there."

"Well, the end had better come quickly. We're under five minutes."

They were. 4:54.

What happened next was a huge surprise.

It began with a thunderous growl—maybe as deep as a lion, and borne on a guttural hiss. Then, about thirty yards in front of them, the thicket rose, then fell, then rose again, like a bubble—then it burst.

A head popped through—thorns and vines, some broken, floated up, thrown to the sky. It was a dragon's head—its eyes as fiery as its flaring nostrils. It looked around for an instant then came to rest on Tim and Kelly. When the dragon saw them it smiled.

As if recognizing an enemy, it belched flame at them.

Kelly backpedaled; Tim merely flinched. The flames fell short.

"We're out of range," Tim said, relieved.

"But we have to get around it!"

"There's no time to plan. We have less than four minutes."

Another belch of flame—red-hot and smoldering.

"Oh, no," Tim gasped.

Kelly saw it too.

The thicket was on fire.

The president's doctor couldn't believe what he was hearing. He stood, mouth open, eyes wide as Terry Baker told him everything.

"Are you sure of all this? We cut him out of there and electricity surges through him? With his heart, it will kill him."

"You're here to see that doesn't happen."

"Medicine is an art—the black bag has no miracles in it." After he stared for a while at the president's black suit he glanced at Tim and Kelly's. Their suits were busy—hands reaching out and grabbing things, like they were swimming or something. "What are those two doing?"

"Who knows? They are not our concern. The president is our concern."

"So you're really going to do this."

"We have to. He's been in there too long already."

The doctor nodded gravely. "Give me a few minutes. I need to turn this place into an emergency room."

"Take all the time you want—five, ten minutes."

"Why are you rushing this?"

"We've got a country to run. And political enemies who want to take it away from us."

The fire in the thicket started as smoke, the residue from the dragon's nasal torch, then erupted into red, dancing flames. It traveled fast. Within seconds it had surrounded the dragon who, with another smile, withdrew its head. And within a few more seconds the flames were heading toward Tim and Kelly.

The snakes didn't like the fire either. They slithered with great speed past the kids, moving lithely, some to the surface where they moved more quickly, some buried deep in the thicket, possibly kept there by their fear.

"The fire's coming, Tim."

Tim said nothing, his brain figuring what to do.

But it was Kelly who set it free. "All the stuff is going up. Everything. Maybe we should go up and hope we land somewhere where we can get to the control room."

"No," Tim said, an idea dawning. "We go down."

Kelly didn't argue. The idea might work. If the flames were going up then they might be able to scramble under them.

But how? The thicket was just that—thick. Digging through the thorns would take forever. And they didn't have forever.

"Look," Tim shouted, the heat from the flames beginning to lap at his hands. Another snake slithered by.

"At what?"

"A hole—sort of."

Kelly saw it. It was a place the thorns and vines had left alone—a hole through the thicket. Not large and with a few thorns. But if they worked fast and smart they might be able to get through it quickly. They had to. Not only was the visor clock ticking away with terrifying speed, but the fire was closing in on them, the sound of it crackling in their ears.

Tim was the first to go through. With legs trailing behind, he made it to the hole. Grabbing thorn after thorn, he pulled himself through. Soon his head emerged from the bottom. The glow of the flames reflected off the ground. As he pulled himself through, his leg caught one of the thorns. He cried out, the pain severe. Cautiously, he set himself free and pulled himself the rest of the way out. After he docked himself in the crotch of several thorns, he allowed himself to rest.

Kelly followed him, and since he'd already cleared the hole of thorns, she slipped through quickly. She stopped beside him.

"I'm not sure we're any better off," she said. "The fire is coming. Pretty soon we're not going to have anything between us and the sky."

"It's leaving some charred vines. Maybe we can hang on to those."

"They'll be hot."

A second or two later they were able to see what would happen. The flames devoured the thicket within a foot, then six inches, then just above them. The heat was intense, but the flames remained above them and never touched them.

The instant the flames passed overhead something else happened. Tim and Kelly dropped like rocks, landing within inches of each other.

The eight-foot drop hurt. But they didn't care. They could run now. Where the thicket had burned away, gravity had returned.

They were down to 3:31 and falling.

Legs still smarting from being stabbed so often, they ran awkwardly at first, but before long they were running for all they were worth. Overhead, what remained of the vines and thorns hung blackened while the thicket before them still burned, the smell acrid.

But none of that mattered. Time was running out, and they still had a long way to go. And they were getting tired and winded.

"All we've done in here is run," Tim said, beginning to do some serious panting. When I get home I'm going down to the lake and spend the rest of the summer lying in the bottom of a boat."

"Do you think Matthew's still helping us?"

"He didn't turn those thorns to rubber."

Suddenly a thunderous roar—a dragon's roar.

But there was no dragon. They could see nothing.

Another roar, and out of the corner of their eyes they saw a burst of smoke and flame—from something tall, from thin air.

"The dragon," Tim said.

"But there's nothing—"

"It's invisible unless it's touching something."

Another roar and another burst of flames and smoke. It remained twenty yards off to their right.

"Can we outrun it?" Kelly asked, her voice anxiously thin.

"We have to try."

Again they took off running—unlike before, the dragon followed, bursts of flame and smoke telling them where it was. It was back there—but gaining.

"I can't take much more of this," Kelly exclaimed breathlessly.

"Keep going. Something will happen. It always does."

They each said a quick prayer as they ran. Although the dragon hadn't coughed fire recently, they knew it was gaining, and they both expected to feel a blowtorch on their necks any second. But it didn't come, and soon they began to believe they were okay—at least for the time being.

They kept running though, their legs becoming rubbery.

"Look, the end of the thicket!" Kelly shouted. "The fire burned through."

It had. Beyond the blackened vines and thorns a world of grassy meadows opened up.

"How much further do you think?"

Tim only shook his head. Although they had only been running a couple of minutes this time, all the scrambling they had done since they had entered VR was catching up to him. What strength remained was draining away.

▣

Equipment of all kinds—breathing machines, heart and brain wave monitors, anything and everything that might be needed to save a heart patient's life was rolled into the White House basement. A small army of technicians all clad in sterile white coats worked feverishly to hook everything up and make sure all was in working order. The president's doctor gravely supervised everything.

"How much longer?" Terry Baker asked the doctor.

"Few minutes." The doctor looked troubled. "I have to ask again. Why are we acting so quickly?"

"Acting slowly would get us to the same place. Every minute is another minute the president's enemies both in the government and out, both in the United States and beyond, can cause us a problem. If a problem occurs while he's locked in there we're all in trouble."

The doctor sighed in unenthusiastic agreement. "Okay, as soon as we finish testing the equipment you can cut him out."

"How long?"

"Two minutes tops."

回

Tim and Kelly burst from beneath the blackened thicket into fresh air. It was like suddenly being free. But they had no time to celebrate. They kept running. Less than two minutes now, and they still had to cross a river somewhere up there.

"There it is!" Kelly exclaimed. They could see the banks of it, the trees lining it. But there was no bridge.

"We can't jump it," Tim cried.

"Maybe we'll see something when we get there."

From somewhere behind them came the roar again—that lion's roar, guttural and immensely threatening.

"You're kidding," Tim groaned, his lungs crying for more and more air.

"Don't look back," Kelly urged, her legs, too, long ago pounded to mush.

The ground shuddered as the invisible dragon took up the chase. Another growl, then a hiss of flames.

Now Tim looked over his shoulder. The flames were erupting from an invisible tower, maybe ten feet tall. The tower was closing in on them.

They reached the river. It wasn't wide, but it was deep, and time seemed to be running faster.

"A rope bridge!" Kelly cried out, pointing.

Tim caught his breath the instant he saw it. A single rope

stretching across the gorge with two hand ropes on either side of it about five feet higher. "One slip and we're hurtin'."

The ground continued to quake as the dragon approached.

"I sure hope he can't jump this thing," Tim mused darkly.

Kelly didn't hear him; she was already balancing herself on the rope bridge. Her hands gripped the guide ropes firmly as she stepped as quickly as possible. She knew that her first slip would be her last, and with it would come the end of her role in the mission.

Tim waited until she was across before he stepped onto the rope.

But he waited too long. Just as he took his first step, a burst of flame flared just behind him—far enough behind that the heat only lapped at his back. But the dragon had to take only a couple more steps and Tim would be toast.

Adrenalin surging through him, Tim did his best to run on the rope. But it was difficult—so difficult that he slipped. Thankfully, his grip on the two hand ropes held. He quickly steadied himself.

"Tim, hurry," Kelly cried.

But he couldn't move any faster and stay on the rope. He expected another blast of flames any second—this one to turn the rope to cinder, dumping him in the canyon.

He heard another roar, this one more distant. Was the dragon leaving?

No—there came another roar from just behind him. Then the earth shuddered, the shudder reverberating up the rope—a dragon was running. Away?

Just as Tim touched solid ground, Kelly saw two dragons collide off in the distance. The furthest one must have drawn off the one about to fry Tim. Now the two of them battled ferociously.

But there was no time to watch.

Less than a minute now—forty-eight seconds and dropping.

"That must be the control room," Tim cried. He pointed to a circular shed in a small grove of trees.

Kelly reached it just behind Tim.

Forty seconds.

Tim stopped in the middle of the circular room and stared at a wall of dials, switches, and monitors. "Which one?"

"Who knows—Lord, which one?"

Thirty-five seconds.

Tim took a calming breath and began reading the labels. The words flew by quickly, one after another.

Twenty-five seconds.

"Here!" Tim cried and dove at the console.

◻

Terry Baker stood beside the president's black suit. Next to him was a Secret Service agent with a sharp blade. Beside him was another agent with a set of long scissors much like hedge clippers. "You guys ready? You make the incision in the front of the suit—you push the clippers in and cut as much and as fast as you can." Then he turned to the other five agents nearby. "And you guys pull that suit off of him." He looked at the doctor. "Ready?"

The doctor stood with five other doctors and nurses. Each was stationed at a different piece of equipment, each ready.

"Okay," Terry said, taking a huge breath. "Cut."

At that instant, Kelly's black suit went limp and her visor lifted. She wasn't sure exactly what she was seeing—men standing around another of the suits preparing to cut into it. But she knew what she had to do. She screamed, and when all the shocked faces turned her way she cried out, "Just push his palm button—push 'em all. All but Tim's that is."

Within seconds the president, his son, and Uncle Morty were all in the process of removing their VR suits. As each of them cheered and looked relieved, Kelly struggled from her black suit. Then, while the doctor pressed close to the president and began asking him questions, the president's son leaned against his father and draped an arm around his waist. Uncle Morty, his heart leaping with the joy of the moment, grabbed Kelly, wrapped his arms around her, and gave her an excited hug. "What a woman—what a woman!"

In the meantime a wall of buffalo came to life and trampled the virtual ground where a moment before the president of the United States, Gar, and Uncle Morty had stood.

The others joined Morty and crowded around Kelly, hugging

her and praising her for coming to their aid. Only after each had expressed his undying appreciation, Uncle Morty asked, "Where's Tim?"

"He'll be out in a second. He had something he wanted to do first."

▣

Tim sat in the circular VR control room at one of the many display terminals. A few minutes before he had pressed several keys on the keyboard and the display had come alive. Now he worked the mouse, investigating the pull-down menus.

Finding one labeled "Characteristics," he selected it.

A stack of names appeared.

He selected "Sonya."

Her characteristics were displayed. Tim leaned back and studied them for a moment. She was five-five, weighed 123, hair black, eyes almond and alive with golden flecks.

"Golden flecks. I'll have to notice those next time."

Age: seventy-five.

*That's the one. How old was she? Eighteen, twenty, twenty-two?*

Tim changed it to twenty. Then he thought for a moment. He stood at a door of opportunity. *Should I take it? You bet!* He changed Sonya's age to fourteen, the same as his, and saved it.

"I can hardly wait to see what that does."

He laughed and pressed his palm button. A moment later VR went dark for him, and his visor opened. Seconds later he joined the excitement. It felt good to give Uncle Morty a hug. It had been a very long day.

# CHAPTER 18

**A**fter spending the night in the White House with Gar and his presidential father, Tim, Kelly, and Uncle Morty flew off the next morning. When they finally landed, Eau Claire airport never looked better. Tim and Kelly's mom and dad met the Secret Service plane, and *they* never looked better. They took turns hugging each of the kids, and even Uncle Morty got a welcome hug before they climbed into the car.

After a few hours of telling and retelling their parents what had happened, Kelly and Tim settled back into their rooms to unpack and unwind. But Kelly could do neither. After unpacking just a few of her clothes, she found the small white rose Gar had given her the night before. It had been part of the centerpiece at dinner, and when he was saying good-bye to her, he took it from a vase and handed it to her. "Just something to remember me by," he had said, his eyes cast down self-consciously. She had taken it and held it all the way back to the hotel. Now she looked at it again and hoped she'd be seeing Gar again soon. He was cute and had great eyes. But more than that, he seemed like a good Christian guy.

Kelly was lost in these thoughts when Tim stepped into her room.

"You still mooning over that rose?" he chided good-naturedly.

Kelly looked up and changed the subject. "We sort of did it again, didn't we?" she said, setting the rose on her desk.

"This one was hard work."

"Virtual Reality is amazing. I wonder how it really works. Do you think we'll ever understand it?"

"I will—someday," Tim said earnestly. "In fact, I want to learn how to program it. I'm going to talk to Uncle Morty tomorrow."

They heard the phone ring downstairs and a moment later their mother's voice, "Kids, Uncle Morty wants you to go over to his farm. Says there's someone there you'll want to see."

Matthew Helbert sat with Uncle Morty on the porch. Both were about the same age, though Matthew looked older with his cloud of premature white hair and pudgier middle. But when he saw the kids running up he leaped to his feet like a kid himself and smiled a broad welcome.

"Dr. Helbert," the kids called in unison the instant they recognized him.

"Tim, Kelly, what a pleasure."

"We were just going in for coffee," Uncle Morty told them. "There's some cookies in the cookie jar."

"Just a Coke will be fine," Tim said, joining them on the porch.

"Same for me."

Around the table, their drinks distributed, Tim said to Matthew, "We owe you big time."

"For what?" Matthew asked.

"You were in VR helping us."

"More than helping us," Kelly said seriously. "Saving our skins."

Morty's brows furled. "You didn't tell me that."

"We were in a hurry. I guess we left some things out," she admitted. "But every time we got into a tight spot something happened to loosen it—snakes drawn away, doors disintegrated . . ."

"Thorns turned to rubber," Tim added.

"Your brother was trying to stop us," Kelly said.

"—hurt us. Maybe even kill us," Tim corrected with emphasis.

"He wanted revenge against us for beating him last time. And you helped us every time."

Matthew said nothing for a moment as if afraid to admit something. But finally he offered, "I came to see how you were doing. I could only track you by address—I was afraid I'd made a mistake."

"You didn't."

"After my horrible mistake with the bacterium and having

used VR to hide the antidote, the courts wouldn't let me nearer to the machine than a thousand miles. I could only help the way I did," he told them. "Was either of you hurt?"

"Scraped up a little," Kelly said. "But that's all."

"That's my machine, yet there's so little of it I know anymore. It was my baby." Matthew looked far away. "My brother's such a gremlin—an evil little gremlin. Dad was right supporting my education over his. All this world needs is a smarter Hammond Helbert."

"He got away too," Uncle Morty said. "He led the Secret Service through some tunnels and escaped."

Matthew's eyes took in Tim, then Kelly. "I knew what he was doing with the machine. When he entered through telecommunications, I did too. I always remained hidden so he wouldn't know I was there, but I followed my machine and him in it as it traipsed from service to service. When it went to the White House and everything started to unfold—especially when you guys came in—I had to do something. Since I had to act so fast all I could think of at the moment was to keep you away from him. I actually wanted to keep all three of you free, but I goofed and only freed you two. As it turned out, you came through just fine."

"Only because of you," Tim reaffirmed.

"And the Lord," Matthew said. "Seeing it all from my end, there were many times when I was guessing—only the Lord could have made all those guesses come out right. And then I had to leave you during the last ten minutes—when Hammond set that timer. I was working on a way to delay it when he cut the transmission cord, and I had to leave you alone."

Kelly looked surprised. "You weren't there during the final bit? With the thorns and the two dragons?"

Now Matthew looked surprised. "Two dragons?" Matthew's brows knit. "I only wrote one. One dragon can't produce an offspring—baby. Hmm. Curious."

"You faced two dragons?" Uncle Morty's mouth suddenly went dry. He took a long drink of coffee.

"One fought the other," Tim explained. "They were too busy to stop us from crossing the rope bridge"

"See," said Matthew with a reassuring smile, "God was in there with us."

The afternoon went quickly, the kids asking Matthew all about VR and Matthew loving the attention. Finally he excused himself and went up to the room Uncle Morty had provided him for the night. A moment later he called down, "What is all this red, white, and blue paint in here for?"

"I'm painting a cow in the morning," Uncle Morty called back.

"I see," said Matthew—really not seeing at all.

"He's cool," Tim said. "I bet he'll help paint."

"He can do the tail," Kelly offered.

"Well, now," Uncle Morty began, "you both believe the Lord does things with a purpose. What do you think he accomplished during this last trip into VR?"

"He brought the president and his son together—for the first time, maybe," Kelly said.

"And the president told us he was going to try to make more godly decisions," Tim added.

"But what about with you?"

"I've been thinking about it, Uncle Morty," Tim said thoughtfully. "Hammond was trying to hurt us, and Matthew was trying to help us. It was like out here. Satan is trying to hurt us; Jesus is working for us. And sometimes when we're in tight places, Jesus pulls us through."

"He pulls us through *all the time*," Uncle Morty said.

"He brings the second dragon," Tim ventured. "Just when the first one is about to burn you to a crisp."

"How did Hammond hurt you?"

They both thought. Tim answered first, "He lied to us in the end. He tricked us."

"He let bad things happen to us," Kelly added. "And he tried to lure us from the straight and narrow. Remember the quicksand?"

"How did Jesus help you through Matthew?" Morty prodded.

"Drew off the bad things so we could escape," Kelly offered.

"He shut the door on us once just before something blew up,"

Tim said, remembering the cross tube in the space station just before A32 blew up.

Uncle Morty's expression became serious. "He taught me something too. Sometimes I rely too much on my own brains and not enough on his love and direction."

"I have this weakness for guys with great eyes," Kelly suddenly admitted. "He used that against me. One of the commandos." Her eyes dropped as if she'd just realized something. "The same thing is happening to me here. I guess I'd better do something about it."

"Bernie? It's me, Kelly."

"Hi, beautiful. You coming over tomorrow to work on the Fourth of July stuff? Come early—we can talk."

Kelly swallowed hard. "No. I just wanted to tell you I won't be helping you."

"Why?"

"I have other plans. I'm helping my uncle. We're painting cows—well, a cow really—but I have high hopes it'll catch on."

"Dad."

John Craft looked up from his workshop bench—pieces of a starter motor lay all over it. "Hi, son. You getting some rest?"

Tim didn't hesitate but launched right in. "You're right about my milk barn computer system. I know just enough to be dangerous sometimes."

"Actually, you know quite a bit. I did pass it by the college. They liked it. It needed some error recovery stuff, and they saw redundancy in some places, but mostly they said it was pretty sound. I was going to talk with you about it tomorrow."

"Really? They liked it?"

"We can talk about how to implement it—I still think you ought to work with somebody."

"Me too. I've got a lot to learn yet."

His father smiled. "Know anything about starter motors?"

"Some."

"Motors have always been a mystery to me. Maybe you

could give me a hand—together we might be able to fix this thing."

回

Kelly slipped into Tim's room after their lights were out. She had found the white rose from Gar on her desk again and had spent a few moments thinking about the time she had spent with him at dinner. But somehow that already seemed long ago and very far away. She was home now where her life really was. But the rose was the key to a wonderful memory. She had set it back on her desk and walked down the hall to Tim's room. There seemed to be more that needed saying, although she wasn't sure what.

Tim wasn't sleeping either but lay in bed staring out through his open window at a starry sky. A warm summer breeze billowed the curtains.

"Jesus really came through for us, didn't he?" she said, sitting on the window seat and marveling at the heavens.

"He's real," Tim said, as if coming to an important conclusion. "It's funny how we have to go into Virtual Reality to see him *really* working with us."

"I guess it's hard to see him working out here. We fight him all the time. But he is at work. And so is the other guy."

"The first dragon," Tim mused gravely.

"Oh, I almost forgot. I asked Bobby Walker to help us paint Elvira tomorrow. He and I had a good talk—he doesn't like to fly either and he's sort of an artist. I suggested we try painting little ads on a few of Dad's cows just to test my theory."

"Cow-Ads—has a ring to it."

"Well," Kelly said, taking a last look at the stars, "see you early. Morty's thinking about painting a whole herd of cows. It'll take most of the day."

"Morty's unreal," Tim said, shaking his head.

"Virtually," Kelly added.

# ABOUT THE AUTHOR

**B**ill Kritlow was born in Gary, Indiana, and moved to northern California when he was nine. He now resides in southern California with his wife, Patricia. They have three daughters and five grandchildren. Bill is also a deacon at his church.

After spending twenty years in large-scale computing, Bill recently changed occupations so that he could spend most of the day writing—his first love. His hobbies include writing, golf, writing, traveling, and taking long walks to think about writing. *The Deadly Maze* follows Bill's first book in the Virtual Reality Series, *A Race Against Time*. He has also written *Driving Lessons* and *Crimson Snow*.

An excerpt from *Backfire,*
Book 3 in the Virtual Reality Series:

◩

Tied to the ancient dead tree at the top of the hill, Princess Kelly cried out, but the White Knight didn't seem to hear her. He had other things on his mind—the Crimson Knight's continued stalking for one.

Again the red guy attacked, again he slammed the White Knight's sword as if he were wielding an ax. Again the White Knight pulled back, but this time, instead of spinning out of the way, the White Knight fell backward. For an instant Kelly's heart stopped. The White Knight couldn't lose! That wasn't possible. She had written it—

Although she had been staring down the hill at the White Knight's plight, she suddenly caught sight of something going on right above her. The sea of black clouds seemed to be gathering just above her head—black, boiling clouds; angry, violent clouds. It was as if they were gathering together all that they had for one last colossal lightning strike. She hadn't written it that way, but she hadn't prevented it either.

She had told the computer she wanted a storm, some lightning, and where she wanted the lightning to strike. The lightning was already striking closer than she wanted; maybe the computer was about to clobber her as well.

It also looked like the Crimson Knight was about to do some clobbering himself. The White Knight was on his back, and the red guy continued to lay into him. With his sword held above his head, the White Knight was holding him off, but only barely.

"I should have created King Kong—he would have just stepped on him," Kelly grumbled.

She looked up. The clouds were still gathering in a huge, inverted bubble. Something was going on up there. And the way things were going, it couldn't be good.